THOROUGHBRED

Ashleigh

LIGHTNING'S
LAST HOPE

JOANNA CAMPBELL

HarperHorizon

An Imprint of HarperCollinsPublishers

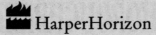
HarperHorizon
An Imprint of HarperCollins*Publishers*
10 East 53rd Street, New York, NY 10022-5299

HarperCollins books are available at special quantity discounts
for bulk purchases for sales promotions, premiums, or fund-raising.
For information please call or write:
Special Markets Department, HarperCollins Publishers, Inc.,
10 East 53rd Street, New York, NY 10022-5299.
Telephone: (212) 207-7528. Fax: (212) 207-7222.

ISBN 0-06-106540-4

HarperCollins® and ■® are trademarks of HarperCollins Publishers, Inc.
Horizon is a registered trademark used under license from Forbes, Inc.

Cover art © 1998 by Daniel Weiss Associates, Inc.

First printing: October 1998

Printed in the United States of America

Visit HarperHorizon on the World Wide Web at
http://www.harpercollins.com

❖ 10 9 8 7 6 5 4 3 2 1

LIGHTNING'S
LAST HOPE

"We've got to help!"

As they rounded the corner of the abandoned barn, Ashleigh gasped. There was a horrible stink, like something rotting. "What's that awful smell?" she asked.

"It smells like something dead," Mona answered.

"Don't say that!" Ashleigh whispered back in alarm.

The smell intensified as they passed the front of the barn. Its door was gaping open, hanging wearily on broken hinges. Ashleigh couldn't resist looking inside to discover the cause of the smell. She let out a cry as she peered into the dim interior. There was a horse in there!

It stood with its head drooping in defeat. The poor animal looked like a living skeleton, with ribs, withers, and hip bones standing out starkly under a shaggy white coat that was streaked with mud. Burrs clung to its long mane and tail. Ashleigh only realized it was alive when the horse lifted its head slowly and looked at them.

"Oh, my gosh!" Ashleigh cried, realizing the stench came from the filthy bedding in the stall. "How could anyone leave an animal in such awful conditions? We've got to help!"

Coming soon:

Ashleigh #2: *A Horse for Christmas*

And collect all the books in the Thoroughbred series:

THOROUGHBRED Super Editions

ASHLEIGH'S Thoroughbred Collection

For Taylor,
my horse-loving granddaughter,
with love

"Life could never get better than this," Ashleigh Griffen sighed.

Every day at Edgardale, her parents' breeding farm sixty miles north of Lexington, Kentucky, was just about perfect. Standing outside the barn early Thursday morning, she gazed out over acres and acres of rolling green pastures divided by pristine white fences. Tall trees shaded the edges of the pastures and lined the gravel drive leading to the Griffens' house and horse barn. It was a beautiful place. But Ashleigh's favorite part was the horses grazing in the spring-green pastures—ten Thoroughbred broodmares, most with young foals at their sides.

Ashleigh grinned as she watched them. Thoroughbreds were the most beautiful creatures on earth. She loved everything about them, even their high-strung behavior and occasional temperamental moods.

Of course, she loved horses of other breeds, too, like her spunky pony, Moe. She and Moe went riding nearly every day with Ashleigh's best friend, Mona Gardner, and Mona's pony, Silver.

When her parents had bought Edgardale, Ashleigh was thrilled to discover that a girl her age lived on the neighboring farm. Well, *almost* her age—Ashleigh had already turned ten, and Mona still had a few months to wait. But since they were in the same class at school and they both loved riding, the girls had quickly become best friends.

"Hey, Ash!" a loud voice called. "Are you planning to stand there all morning?"

Ashleigh stuck out her tongue at her thirteen-year-old sister, Caroline. Taking one last look at the mares, she followed Caroline into the barn to start her morning chores. Every day Ashleigh had to muck out four stalls. Caroline did four different stalls, and their five-year-old brother, Rory, had just gotten his first mucking-out assignment this month.

While the kids worked, their parents tended to the horses. Since Edgardale was still a small and struggling operation, the Griffens could afford only one hired hand, Kurt Bradley. Kurt was a quiet man who seemed to like horses better than he liked people. He lived in the small apartment on the second floor of the barn.

Ashleigh didn't mind the hard work. It was worth it to live on a farm with such amazing horses. She set to work, pitching soiled bedding out of her first stall into a wheelbarrow in the barn aisle. When the barrow was full, she pushed it outside to the manure pile near the Griffens' vegetable garden. Ashleigh's mother had already started preparing the bed for seeding, using the manure as fertilizer.

Back in the barn, Ashleigh headed toward her next stall. Suddenly she was showered by a forkful of dirty bedding. She stopped in her tracks and glared into the adjoining stall.

"Caro!" she cried. "You did that on purpose!"

A blond head appeared above the stall's half door. Caroline and Rory took after their fair-haired mother, while Ashleigh had her father's darker coloring.

"Did not!" Caroline protested, but her accompanying giggle told a different story. "I just have bad aim."

"Sure!" Ashleigh plucked pieces of smelly straw from her shoulder-length hair. "Yuck! Now my hair is filthy. I'll get you for this, Caro."

"Oh, I'm scared," Caroline mocked her.

Ashleigh angrily continued up the aisle. She'd have just enough time to finish her chores before hurrying in to change for school. She'd hoped to have a little extra time that morning to go out to the paddock fence and visit the foals. Instead, she'd have to take another shower to wash her hair.

Finishing up, Ashleigh stowed the pitchfork and wheelbarrow in the storage room at the end of the barn. Her parents came in from the paddocks. Her dad looked at his watch and raised his eyebrows at Ashleigh.

"You'd better get a move on, young lady, or you'll miss the bus," he said, ruffling her hair.

"I know, Dad. I just finished."

"Well, you're a big help in the barn, but school's important, too."

Ashleigh nodded her acknowledgment but wished it weren't so. Not that she disliked school, but helping care for the horses was so much more fun.

"Your lunch is in the fridge," her mother said, smiling. "And send Rory down to the barn before you leave."

"I will, Mom." Ashleigh set off at a run for the house, slamming through the back door into the kitchen, then heading for the stairs and her room.

Caroline was already dressed and preening in front of her full-length mirror. Ashleigh dug through the pile of clothes strewn across her own side of the room in search of her favorite jeans. Caroline looked over her shoulder and shook her head.

"Ash, are you *ever* going to get more organized?" Caroline was as neat as Ashleigh was messy. She never had trouble finding her own clothes, because they were always hung up in the closet.

Ashleigh just shook her head distractedly as she searched through her dresser drawers. She finally found her jeans under the bed, but by then Caroline had claimed the bathroom. Ashleigh grabbed up her change of clothes and pounded on the door. "Hurry up, Caro. I still have to take a shower."

"That's your problem," Caroline called back.

"It wouldn't have been if you hadn't thrown muck all over me!"

The words were barely out of her mouth when the door cracked open. "All right, Your Highness, it's all yours," Caroline said with a smile.

Ashleigh grimaced and pushed through into the bathroom. There were times when she felt like strangling her sister, and this was one of them. Ten minutes later she rushed back into the bedroom for her backpack.

"Ashleigh," Caroline cried, "you're not going to go to school looking like that, are you?"

Ashleigh glanced down at her shirt and jeans. "Like what?"

"Your shirt is so wrinkled, it looks like you slept in it."

"I don't have time to change. Where did I leave my hairbrush?"

"On the bathroom sink."

"Thanks." Ashleigh rushed in that direction, dragged the brush through her hair, then pounded down the stairs, yelling to her brother, "Rory, Mom wants you out in the barn."

"I'm going," he called from his own room.

Ashleigh reached the end of the drive just as the bus was approaching. Caroline's bus to the middle/high school complex wouldn't arrive for another few minutes, and Rory was in afternoon kindergarten, so their mother drove him to school.

Mona was seated in their usual spot, and Ashleigh breathlessly slid in beside her. Mona grinned at Ashleigh's frazzled appearance. "Late again?" she asked.

For an instant Ashleigh frowned. Then she giggled. "I know. My shirt's a wrinkled mess. Caro told me all about it, but I didn't have time to change. Anyway, by lunch the wrinkles will be gone."

"Sometimes I'm glad I'm an only child," Mona replied. "My mother has time to get my stuff ready for me."

"Yeah, I guess it's pretty hard for my parents sometimes, with three kids and so many horses," Ashleigh said. "But I wish I could be doing what they're doing instead of going to school."

"Someday we both will be," Mona said, "when we have our own farms."

Ashleigh's eyes brightened at that happy thought just as the bus hit a bump and her backpack slid off her lap. Her math workbook fell out and landed open on the floor. Mona reached down for it and sighed when she saw the empty page.

"Ashleigh, you didn't do your math homework again."

Ashleigh made a face. "I started . . . but there was this incredible article in this month's *Blood Horse*—"

"And you read it instead of doing your homework."

"It was so interesting! A lot more interesting than dumb long division, and by the time I was done reading, I was so tired. . . ." Ashleigh's voice drifted off. She knew her excuse was lame. "I was going to do the homework problems during homeroom and lunch."

"Ash, you know what your parents are going to say if you get another bad grade in math."

"I know." Ashleigh didn't want to think about the riding privileges she'd lose. "Don't worry, I'll get it done." She took the workbook from Mona and shoved it into her backpack. "I think it's going to be nice this afternoon. Do you want to come over and ride? We could go up to the spring where the deer drink. And after that, we can play with the foals. Jolita's little filly is so cute! She and Slewette's filly have been ganging up on all the guys."

"Math, Ash," Mona said, "that's what you need to concentrate on." Then she laughed. "Yeah, let's go riding. I'll bring Silver over, and maybe afterward I'll have time to help you with your math homework."

"Would you?" Ashleigh cast her friend a grateful smile. Mona was a whiz at math, the only subject Ashleigh truly hated. With Mona's help, she'd have her homework done twice as fast, and they'd be able to spend more time riding.

When the bus pulled up at school, Ashleigh spotted Lynne and Jamie waiting by the front door. The two girls loved horses almost as much as Ashleigh and Mona did.

"Hi, you guys," she called, getting off the bus. Mona followed her over.

"Hey, Ash, nice shirt," Lynne said with a grin.

Ashleigh rolled her eyes. "I know, I know. Let's hurry to homeroom so I can do my math homework," she said.

"Are you two going riding this afternoon?" Jamie asked as they headed down the crowded hallway. When they both nodded, she added, "You're so lucky.

You can ride at your own place. I have to wait until my mom has time to take me to the stable."

Jamie and Lynne both had ponies but couldn't keep them at home, since they lived in town.

"But you said your parents are getting you a horse for your birthday, Lynne," Mona reminded her. "You'll be the first of us to graduate from pony to horse. And Jamie gets to go to Keeneland all the time because her father calls races and gets free clubhouse passes. Wouldn't Ashleigh and I love that!"

Ashleigh smiled, remembering the times her parents had taken the whole family to Churchill Downs, Keeneland, or Turfway Park. She'd loved every moment, especially the time spent roaming around the backside seeing the horses up close and talking to various trainers and other breeders. Of course, her family could only afford to go on special occasions when one of their former charges was running.

Someday, Ashleigh thought, *I'll be a jockey and I'll spend all my time at a racetrack. And no one will make me do math homework!*

When she got home that afternoon, Ashleigh found her mother at the sink doing dishes. "Hi, Mom," Ashleigh called brightly. "How are the babies?"

"The babies are doing fine. You and Mona are going riding?"

"How did you know?" Ashleigh asked in surprise.

Her mother laughed and pushed a blond strand of hair off her forehead with the back of her wrist. "Ashleigh, after ten years, I think I can read your expressions. Whenever your eyes are dancing like they are right now, you've got something fun planned. You're just like your father. Have fun, but don't be out too late. You have homework, I'm sure."

"Mona's helping me with it."

"That's good news."

Ashleigh bounded up the stairs to change into work jeans and riding boots. She knew it would take Mona about a half hour to change, tack up Silver, and get to the farm. Ashleigh had the bedroom to herself, since Caroline wasn't home yet.

Caroline was probably doing stuff with her friends in town after school. Most of the time Ashleigh just didn't understand her older sister. Caroline could ride and knew horse care, but she wasn't interested. She would rather spend hours looking through teen magazines with her friends than be at the farm with the horses. It mystified Ashleigh.

A few minutes later Ashleigh rushed from the house. Moe was grazing in his own small paddock adjoining the broodmares'. He pretended not to see Ashleigh as she approached. Only his ears flicking back in her direction betrayed that he had heard her coming. Ashleigh was the first to admit that Moe could be lazy, especially when faced with the choice between lush grass and work. She stood by the fence for a few minutes, lead rope in hand, chuckling as she watched him. Moe, never lifting his head, sneaked a wily look in her direction, then moved determinedly to the far-thest end of the paddock.

"I know your tricks, Molasses," she called. "You're not fooling me." He'd gotten his name from the brown coloring of his coat, not from his lazy disposi-tion. Ashleigh's parents, who had inherited Moe when they bought the farm, suspected Moe had quite a bit of Welsh pony mixed in with his otherwise Shetland genes. Though long-maned and -tailed, he was tall for a Shetland, standing just under thirteen hands at his shoulder, and was finer-boned. Welsh ponies were one of the most refined of the pony breeds, while Shetlands were one of the most hardy. Still, despite Moe's height, Ashleigh was rapidly outgrow-ing him. She wasn't especially tall for her age, but she longed for a bigger and more powerful mount.

A Thoroughbred, she thought longingly, or even a mixed breed—any horse who would have the heart of

Moe, yet have the power to do great things. That would be her start, but someday she wanted to jockey Thoroughbreds like the ones they raised at Edgardale and to win races with them.

They didn't have any pleasure horses at Edgardale, although Ashleigh's parents, who were excellent riders, sometimes rode the mares over the grassy lanes at Edgardale. The mares had all been trained for racing, and several had had moderately impressive race records before being retired. They enjoyed getting out and stretching their legs. But her parents rarely rode the mares except in late summer or during the fall, when the previous year's foals were mature enough to be left alone and the mares weren't so far advanced into their next pregnancy that riding them would pose any risk.

There was one foal, though, Ashleigh remembered, who'd actually crawled *under* the paddock fence when he saw his mother jogging off into the distance with Mrs. Griffen on her back. He'd followed them, loping behind, until the ride was finished.

Ashleigh brought her mind back to the present. "Okay, Moe, game time's over," she said, opening the paddock gate. From her pocket she removed several sugar cubes. If there was one thing Moe loved above all else, it was sugar cubes. She set out across the pasture toward him.

He watched from the corner of his eye but stayed where he was, head bent to the grass. As she drew within a few yards of him, Ashleigh sensed indecision in the pony. She held out her hand, sugar cubes on her palm. The temptation was just too great. Moe lifted his head, sniffed, and stared at her hand. When Ashleigh was within grabbing distance of Moe's halter, she extended her arm fully. Moe couldn't resist. He lipped up the treat from her palm, giving her enough time to take a firm hold on his halter. He chomped and rolled the sugar cubes around in his mouth as Ashleigh clipped on the lead line.

Before she led him off, Moe gave her a sardonic look that said, *Okay, you got me, but you cheated. Wait till next time.* Ashleigh patted his neck affectionately.

The funny thing about Moe was that once he was caught, he was a perfectly agreeable mount, ready for anything. Ashleigh led him back to the barn and put him in crossties, then went to the tack room to collect his saddle and bridle. She had just finished buckling the cheek strap on his bridle when she heard Silver's hoofbeats coming down the drive. Ashleigh led Moe outside and waved to Mona.

Silver was a purebred Welsh and got his name from his coloring, although at age eighteen he was now pure white, with just a few indistinct gray dapples.

Ashleigh grinned at Mona, fastened her riding helmet, flipped the reins over Moe's head, and swung into the English saddle. Mona was similarly mounted in English saddle. "Ready?" Ashleigh asked Mona.

Mona grinned back. "Let's ride."

2

The girls headed up one of the grassy lanes between the paddocks. Everything seemed fresh and new in the soft spring sunshine.

"I love this time of year," Ashleigh said happily, "except that we're still in school."

Mona chuckled. "Only a couple of months before summer vacation."

The ponies were enjoying the spring air, too. They eagerly picked up the pace when the girls asked them to trot.

"I found a new shortcut to the spring," Ashleigh said. "It's a little rough in places, but do you want to try it?"

Mona looked over with a smile. "Sure. I'm always ready for an adventure."

"It should be right up here," Ashleigh said, studying the line of woodland above the pastures. "There it is."

She heeled Moe forward. "Let me go first. It's kind of tight."

Moe didn't hesitate entering the narrow path into the woods. "I think it may be a deer trail," Ashleigh called over her shoulder to Mona. "It leads straight to the spring." Ashleigh slowed Moe's pace to a walk over the rougher ground. The soil beneath the ponies' hooves was moist and soft from the recent spring rains.

"Look for deer tracks, Ash. There should be some in this soft ground."

Ashleigh did as her friend instructed, peering at the shaded trail ahead, looking for the distinctive cloven prints. "There's one!" she cried. "And there are some more. Wow! A couple of the prints are really big. I'll bet they're from a buck." She pulled up so that Mona could move Silver up beside her on the narrow path and get a good look herself.

"Yup," Mona agreed. "Some of those prints were definitely made by a buck, and they look fresh. Maybe they're still at the spring. Let's be real quiet so we don't startle them."

Ashleigh nodded, and they moved on at a walk, single file, not making a sound. Even the ponies' hoof-beats were muffled by the damp ground.

The path was by no means straight. It curved

around patches of dense brush, winding through shaded woodland. Then Ashleigh spotted the clearing up ahead. She turned to Mona and put a finger to her lips. The girls and their ponies were still hidden by the trees. They moved forward slowly and stopped at the edge of the clearing. At the far side was the spring, which bubbled out of the rocks to form a sparkling pool.

Two does stood drinking the water. Each had a tiny fawn at her side. And standing just behind them, his head alertly raised, was a huge buck. His new rack was growing and would continue to grow until fall and rutting season. Then the felt covering would fall from his rack, and he would do battle with other bucks for control of the does.

Ashleigh held her breath as she and Mona watched the beautiful animals. The buck was a magnificent sight. And the fawns were so sweet with their spotted coats and oversized ears and legs. They reminded Ashleigh of the foals on the farm.

Moe, quietly patient until then, snorted. It was a soft snort, but the buck's hearing was acute. He made a huffing noise at the does. In a blink of an eye they had all turned, their white tails raised in alarm, and were off silently into the woods. The girls could only stare after them.

"Cool," Mona said. "Boy, would my dad like to know about that buck. He'd be a trophy come hunting season."

"You're not going to tell him!" Ashleigh cried in alarm.

"Of course not," Mona assured her. "Besides, your land is posted. He couldn't hunt here anyway."

The girls walked the ponies around the edge of the pool to where the deer had been drinking. From the number of prints in the mud, it was clear that the deer came often. Ashleigh turned to the spot where they'd disappeared into the woods. "Look, the trail goes on up the hill," she said.

"Let's follow it," Mona suggested.

Ashleigh considered. "If we do, we won't get back in time to play with the foals. My parents bring them in about four-thirty. We can follow it another day when we have more time. Maybe Saturday."

"Good idea."

On the way back, once out of the woods, they raced each other down one of the lanes. Mona won. Moe did his best, but Silver, being a full-bred Welsh, had longer legs. Both girls were exhilarated when they pulled the ponies up.

"You won't beat me so easily when I have my own horse," Ashleigh said. "No offense, Moe," she added, patting the pony's neck. "I'm just outgrowing you, and if I'm going to train to be a jockey, I'll need a bigger horse."

"Like a Thoroughbred," Mona said.

"Preferably a filly—and one who could win the Kentucky Derby."

Mona laughed. "You've got such an imagination, Ashleigh. You're always making up these stories like they're going to come true."

"Maybe they will. Anyway, it doesn't hurt to dream."

Once back at the barn, they untacked the ponies. Mona put Silver into one of the empty stalls until she was ready to ride home again. Ashleigh put Moe back in the paddock. She knew she'd have no trouble catching him to bring him in later, since it would be his dinnertime. He'd probably be waiting at the gate.

They walked over to the paddocks holding the mares and foals. Since a couple of the mares didn't get along with each other, always feuding over who was "boss" mare, the Griffens had separated them, putting the bossy ones, like My Georgina, into paddocks with less aggressive mares. They also kept the youngest foals and their dams in a separate one-acre paddock until the babies had matured enough to fend for themselves against the older foals.

That's where Ashleigh and Mona went now. "That's Jolita's filly . . . the one I said was so cute," Ashleigh said, pointing to a fuzzy, long-legged foal grazing beside her dam. "She looks like she's going to be a chestnut like her mom. She's only a week old, but she's full of it. And that little bay filly is Slewette's."

They heard running footsteps behind them, and a second later Rory joined them at the fence. "Are you going to play with the foals, Ash?" His reddish blond hair was tousled, and he had a smudge of dirt on his cheek. Rory loved horses as much as Ashleigh and, having grown up around them, he had absolutely no fear. He had started learning to ride on Moe when he was three, but their parents wouldn't let him ride out on the trails yet unless they were with him.

"We were thinking about it," Ashleigh answered teasingly. Rory wasn't allowed to go into the paddocks alone, either.

"Come on, Ash?" he pleaded.

She grinned down at him. "Yeah, let's go." They let themselves into the paddock, carefully latching the gate behind them. They'd been taught at an early age not to be careless with gates—horses were no fun to catch. Besides, the animals were valuable and could easily injure themselves running loose.

Ashleigh gave a whistle. Both foals picked up their

heads and looked in her direction. Their dams continued grazing, undisturbed as the foals ambled over to the kids. The mares were familiar with Ashleigh and Rory and knew their foals were safe. They wouldn't have acted so disinterested if a stranger had entered the paddock.

"Hey, cuties," Ashleigh said, kneeling down to hug the littlest. "Want to play tag?"

The foal nuzzled her head against Ashleigh's chest, pushing at Ashleigh with her tiny muzzle.

Mona and Rory cuddled the bay foal, who was slightly larger. "Have you named them yet, Ash?" Mona asked.

"Pip and Tip," Ashleigh said. "I'm running out of nicknames."

"I named two of the foals in the other paddock," Rory boasted. "I'm making a list of names for next year. Mom's writing them down for me."

"I don't know how you keep them all straight," Mona said.

"It's easy when you see them every day," Ashleigh replied. "And they're all a little bit different. Of course, these won't be their official names."

Mona nodded. "I still don't understand how you can bear to see them sold when they're yearlings."

"They go to good owners," Rory piped up.

"Mommy and Daddy make sure of that."

"And we check up on them when they're racing and stuff," Ashleigh added, but her smile disappeared for a moment. It did hurt to have to say goodbye to the babies she'd helped raise for over a year, but the farm wouldn't make any money if they didn't sell their yearlings. When the yearlings left Edgardale—some sold privately, others sold at reputable Thoroughbred auctions—they were fit, healthy, well mannered, and trained to halter and lead line.

"Besides, at least the mares stay at the farm. We never have to say goodbye to *them*," Ashleigh said. She shook her head, trying to clear the sad thoughts. "Let's play. Hey, Pip, bet you can't catch me!"

Ashleigh set off across the grass with the smallest filly in pursuit. Mona and Rory raced off in opposite directions, leaving the larger foal, Tip, very confused about whom she was supposed to chase. Finally she used her superior speed to catch them both, first racing toward Rory and running a circle around him, then bounding across the paddock to catch Mona.

The foals, awkward though they were, usually won the contest against their human friends, although they liked the play so much that they often loped along beside their human playmates, only putting on a burst of speed at the last minute. When Ashleigh, Mona, and

Rory were all winded, they plopped down on the grass, laughing as the foals nuzzled their clothing and hair trying to get them back on their feet for more play.

Mona left just before dinner, saddling and riding Silver the short distance back to her house. With Mona's help, Ashleigh had finished her math homework in record time. She'd also begun to feel less intimidated by the problems after Mona explained some of the basics Ashleigh had missed in class. She had to admit that she'd probably been daydreaming about horses when the teacher had explained them.

"See you Saturday?" Mona asked as she mounted Silver.

"Definitely!" Ashleigh agreed. "I can't wait to see what we find on the deer trail."

3

Ashleigh woke on Saturday morning with a tingle of anticipation. She sat up in bed and turned to look out the window. The sun was shining, and the sky was nearly cloudless—a perfect day for a long ride. She threw her legs over the side of the bed and hunted for her slippers. Caroline was still sound asleep. Ashleigh took care not to wake her as she gathered up a sweat-shirt, jeans, and boots and headed toward the bath-room.

After she showered and dressed, she breezed through the kitchen, where her mother was preparing a big Saturday morning breakfast. "Morning, Mom."

"Good morning, Ash. Make sure you come in for breakfast after your chores, or I'll come and get you."

"Don't worry, Mom. I have to come in and pack a lunch anyway. Mona and I are going for a trail ride."

Once in the barn, Ashleigh cleaned her stalls in

record time. Caroline and Rory were only half finished when she put away her pitchfork. True to her word, she returned to the house for a breakfast of French toast smothered in maple syrup. She cleared away her dishes and went to the fridge to get the ingredients for sandwiches. She made two each for herself and Mona, wrapped them, then ran upstairs for her backpack. She filled it with sandwiches, fruit, a big bag of chips, and two bottles of water. Then she lugged it out to the barn and went to get Moe.

Her father had put the pony out in his paddock, so Ashleigh had to use the sugar cube trick to catch him. "We're going to have so much fun today, Moe. We're going to go exploring and have a picnic, and maybe we'll even see the deer again."

Moe snorted with total disinterest, but Ashleigh knew his attitude would change once they were out on the trails. The night before, she'd given his tack a good cleaning, so now it had the clean smell of saddle soap. Putting the pony in crossties, she groomed him carefully. He'd lost most of his shaggy winter coat, but Ashleigh used the scraper to remove the last remaining tufts.

In the summer she could brush his coat to a lovely shine, but for now she had to settle for something slightly short of that. After brushing the tangles from his long mane and tail, she got the hoof pick and carefully cleaned his unshod feet, picking out all the caked mud.

Since she and Mona would be riding all day, Ashleigh decided to wear the leather chaps she had stored in the tack room. She laid a clean, fluffy white saddle pad on Moe's back, then lifted his English saddle, positioning it carefully before buckling the girth. She wouldn't put his bridle on until Mona arrived.

With time on her hands, Ashleigh left Moe in the crossties and wandered out to the paddocks. She walked along the white fences admiring the mares— the black beauty, Wanderer, who consistently produced outstanding foals; the bays, Marvy Mary, Slewette, and Zip Away; the chestnuts, Jolita, My Georgina, and Althea; and the three whites, Impish Gal, Go Gen, and Prospector's Mine.

"Hey, Ash!" Mona called. Ashleigh turned to see her friend and Silver trotting down the drive. She hurried over to meet them.

"Great day for a ride," Mona said with a grin.

"Sure is," Ashleigh agreed. "Moe's all ready except for his bridle. It'll only take me a sec."

"I'll go watch the foals till you're ready," Mona said, dismounting and leading Silver in that direction.

Ashleigh put on her hard hat, fastened the chin strap, then stuck her arms through the straps of her backpack. She quickly bridled Moe and led him out of the barn. Mona saw her and led Silver back from the paddocks.

"Okay, expedition ready?" Ashleigh said in mock military tones. "Mount up!" And when they both were in the saddle, "Forward march!"

They started off at a walk, but once they were past the lower paddock fences, they urged the ponies into a ground-covering trot.

"Do you still want to follow the deer trail past the spring?" Mona asked.

"Definitely. Have you changed your mind?"

"No way," Mona answered. "Who knows what we'll find? You said your parents never come up here. Maybe we'll find an old Indian camp or something."

Ashleigh began to laugh, then was caught by Mona's imaginative mood. "Right. Maybe we will."

They set off along the same route as their last ride, following the grassy paddock lanes until they reached the break in the woods where the deer trail started. As before, they moved as quietly as they could. The ground had dried over the last few days, so the deer prints weren't as evident, but that didn't mean the deer weren't by the pool.

As they edged up to the clearing and spotted the pool, they saw that the same deer were there, drinking: the two does and their fawns, and the huge buck watching over them.

Neither the girls nor the ponies made a sound, but something alerted the buck to their presence. He threw up his head, scenting the air. Ashleigh didn't know whether they were upwind or downwind from the deer, but an instant later the buck sounded the alert. The does lifted their heads in alarm, turned to their fawns, and within seconds the whole group had disappeared into the woods.

For a moment Ashleigh and Mona stared. Then they heeled their ponies forward.

"We have to follow them this time," Mona said.

"I don't think we'll catch them," Ashleigh answered, urging Moe through the muddy edge of the pool. "But maybe we can see where they go."

The ponies were game as the girls urged them up the deer trail at the other end of the spring-fed pool. The route was just as narrow as the path they'd followed in. They couldn't go too quickly, because there were branches to be avoided and roots jutting out underfoot. The deer had flown over the debris. The girls had to be more cautious.

"Maybe we'll find the place where they bed down,"

Mona called. "My father says it's usually under a bunch of pine trees, or in a thicket."

They continued on and soon reached a fork where two clear deer trails led off in different directions. "Which way?" Mona asked. They both studied the ground, but there were tracks in the hardened mud on both paths.

"You decide," Ashleigh said. "Whichever way you pick, I'll break a branch as a marker."

"Good idea," Mona said. "Let's go to the right. The path goes uphill."

Ashleigh reached up and snapped a slender branch overhanging the path, leaving the broken end dangling. They continued on, both intent on the chase. They hit another fork, and Ashleigh broke a second branch.

After about ten minutes, they found a tiny clearing where a small brook rippled and gurgled down the hill. "I bet this is where the spring comes from," Ashleigh said. "Let's have lunch here."

Mona nodded. "I'm starving, but this is fun. I feel like I'm an explorer, like Lewis and Clark," she added as she dismounted.

History was one subject Ashleigh did like, and that year their teacher had had them watch a videotaped television series about Lewis and Clark exploring the West, linking it to their regular classwork. She and Mona tied up the ponies and settled on the grass to wolf down their sandwiches and snacks and quench their thirst.

Ashleigh breathed in the fresh air as she listened to the splashing brook and the merry chirp of birds in the trees. How she loved the outdoors, especially when they were doing something exciting.

The girls stayed in the clearing for a while, knowing that they'd never catch the deer, but still hoping to find them. Finally Ashleigh rose and stretched. "Ready to head out again?" she asked Mona.

"I wonder how far this trail goes," Mona mused as she swung her leg over Silver's back and settled into her saddle. "Do you think we're still on your parents' property?"

"I don't know," Ashleigh said. "I've never gone this far into the woods before. I'm not sure where our property ends, but as long as we stay on the trail, we'll be fine."

They continued following the trail they'd been on, uphill and down through the woods. They waded through a couple of seasonal brooks, where they again saw prints of the buck and his family in the mud.

"We're getting closer," Mona whispered.

"I think we are," Ashleigh agreed. "These prints look fresh. I hope we won't scare them."

They'd taken another fork in the trail, following the prints. Then suddenly the tracks disappeared up a grassy rise. The trail they were on still snaked forward through the woods, but the deer hadn't followed it, and there was no way the girls could track the deer through the thick meadow grass. Ashleigh and Mona looked at each other.

"What do we do now?" Mona asked.

"I don't know," Ashleigh said.

"Maybe we should turn back," Mona suggested. "It's probably getting late, and you have your afternoon chores to do."

"I guess we should," Ashleigh agreed. "It's a bummer that we didn't find them, but it still was fun." She turned Moe and gazed back along the path. The landscape looked different all of a sudden; the woods seemed thicker and darker. Ashleigh urged Moe forward, retracing the hoofprints she could clearly see in the soft ground. Mona followed. Then suddenly the hoofprints faded. They'd reached an area where the ground was dry and leaf covered. Not only that, but the path branched out into three separate trails.

"I don't remember this," Ashleigh said in confusion.

"I don't either," Mona agreed. "But you marked the branches. There must be a broken one here somewhere."

Ashleigh's face fell. "Oh, no. Oh, Mona, I'm sorry, but I was having so much fun, I didn't bother to mark the last couple of turns. I didn't think we'd have any trouble finding our way back. But it all looks so different."

Mona stared at her. "Then what are we going to do?"

Ashleigh, feeling responsible, tried to think. They didn't know which of the three paths they'd taken, and following the wrong one could get them in worse trouble. Ashleigh calculated that they were pretty high up on the hill that rose above Edgardale and several neighboring farms. They needed to go downhill to get to the main road or Edgardale's pastures.

She turned Moe again. "Maybe we should just keep going," she said. "This path leads downhill. The others don't. It's got to take us someplace that we'll recognize."

Mona looked worried, but she nodded. "Okay, but don't forget to mark the trail this time. I'll mark it, too, just in case."

Mona turned Silver, and they both continued down the path, passing the spot where the deer had bounded into the field. Then they rode on into new territory. Ashleigh prayed she'd made the right decision. She didn't want to make her parents angry, and she sure didn't want to be in the woods at night. She was also beginning to feel frightened.

They were lost!

4

"This trail has got to take us down to the nearest road," Ashleigh said, trying to reassure herself as well as Mona.

Mona was silent, which didn't reassure Ashleigh at all.

The trail obviously had been used by deer, although there were no fresh tracks. It was narrow, and the girls had to keep pushing aside branches. The path continued to descend, though, which was one encouraging thing. Ashleigh just hoped it continued all the way down to safety and didn't peter out into nothing.

Time seemed to drag as the ponies trudged on under the leafy canopy. The spring growth totally obscured her view now, and Ashleigh wondered how she could have considered the green leaves so beautiful that morning. She couldn't see anything beyond the trees.

"Ash, I'm scared," Mona said.

Ashleigh didn't dare admit that she was afraid, too. "We can't panic, Mona. We're going to find a way home."

She hoped she was right.

For another half hour they rode down the narrow path. "Look, Ash!" Mona suddenly shouted. "There's a clearing up ahead. I can see the sun."

Relief flooded through Ashleigh's veins. If there was a clearing, it could only mean a farm or a road.

They trotted out of the darkness of the woods and stopped.

In front of them was a ramshackle farmhouse and barn, and a fenced pasture where more weeds grew than grass. The grounds were littered with junked cars and car parts, and the place looked deserted. In fact, Ashleigh couldn't imagine anyone living in the sag-roofed house, where the paint was peeling off every board. The barn looked just as bad.

"What a mess," Mona whispered.

Ashleigh felt the need to whisper, too. There was something about the place that sent a shiver up and down her spine. "Maybe there's a drive to the road on the other side of the house," she suggested, sounding braver than she felt. "If we circle around the barn to the front, maybe we can find it."

"We don't have much choice unless we turn around," Mona said, "and I am definitely not going back into the woods!"

They walked the ponies forward, edging along the pasture fence and around the side of the barn. Ahead they saw a rutted drive leading off through the woods in the front of the house.

"Whew," Ashleigh said with relief. "Our way out." Then, as they rounded the corner of the barn, she gasped. There was a horrible stink, like something rotting. "What's that awful smell?" she asked.

"It smells like something dead," Mona answered, wrinkling her nose.

"Don't say that!" Ashleigh whispered back in alarm.

The smell intensified as they passed the front of the barn. Its door was gaping open, hanging wearily on broken hinges. Although Ashleigh intended to bolt down the drive leading away from the forlorn property as quickly as possible, she couldn't resist looking inside to discover the cause of the smell.

She let out a cry as she peered into the dim interior. There was a horse in there!

It stood with its head drooping in defeat. The poor animal looked like a living skeleton, with ribs, withers, and hip bones standing out starkly under a shaggy white coat that was streaked with mud. Burrs clung to its long mane and tail. The horse lifted its head slowly and looked at them.

"Oh, my gosh!" Ashleigh cried, realizing the stench came from the filthy bedding in the stall.

"What's a horse doing here?" Mona cried. "Do you think someone actually lives here? The whole place looks abandoned."

"Well, if someone does live here, they're starving this horse! How could anyone leave an animal in such awful conditions? We've got to help."

Ashleigh dismounted, tied Moe's reins to a nearby sapling, and strode toward the barn. Mona was right behind her.

The interior of the barn was as cluttered and filthy as the yard. Aside from the small open stall where the horse stood, the first floor was crammed with boxes, broken machinery, and litter. There was a rickety loft where a few bales of hay were stored.

Quietly the two girls approached the horse. On closer inspection, they could see it was a mare between fifteen and sixteen hands tall. Despite her decrepit appearance, her conformation was excellent, with long legs and a finely shaped head. But the brown eyes that stared back at them were dull and lifeless.

"You poor baby," Ashleigh said softly, stepping closer and raising her arm to lay a gentle hand on the mare's bony back. The mare didn't react to the touch or make a sound.

"Her spirit's broken," Mona murmured sadly.

"Or she's weak from not being fed. Look, you can see every one of her ribs, and she can't have been groomed in months."

Ashleigh looked down at the deplorable bedding in the stall. The stall couldn't have been cleaned in months, either, and had attracted swarms of flies. Even the mare stood as far away from the filth as the length of the rope attached to her halter would allow. "There's nothing here for her to eat."

"And her water's all scummy, too," Mona added angrily.

The mare turned her head and gazed at Ashleigh. "She almost looks like she's pleading with us to help," Ashleigh said mournfully.

Her instincts told her that she *had* to help. Everything she'd ever been taught led her to believe that suffering animals needed human help.

"We've got to get her out of here," Ashleigh said, reaching to unhook the lead rope attached to the wall of the stall. She gently backed the mare out of her stall and turned her toward the open door. Then she and

Mona led the mare out onto the sunlit drive. The mare made no protest. Her will seemed to have been sapped away by long-term neglect.

"There's a patch of grass over there," Ashleigh said, leading the mare in that direction. "I'm going to let her graze for a while. Why don't you get the ponies?" she added to Mona.

"Right." Mona hurried over to untie the two ponies.

"And just what do you think you're doing?" a loud voice demanded.

Ashleigh spun around to see a man pointing a shotgun at them. He had stringy gray hair and was sloppily dressed, and his expression was frightening. "Trying to steal my horse?" he asked.

Ashleigh stared at the man's gun. "No—" she began, then stopped when she realized that was exactly what she had been doing, except that she hadn't thought of it that way. "We—We were t-trying to help her," she stammered.

"By stealing her right out of her stall?" he asked bitingly.

"She didn't have any food and—" Ashleigh choked off her words when she saw the man's angry scowl deepen.

"How I take care of my horse is my business! You're

trespassing, and I don't abide trespassers—especially thieving ones!"

"W-We were lost," Ashleigh tried to explain.

"And finding your way back home, you ended up in my barn?" The man snorted. "We'll see what the police have to say about that!"

Mona gasped. "Please, no! We didn't think—"

"I guess you didn't." He motioned to Ashleigh with his gun. "Put the mare back in her stall," he ordered.

Ashleigh felt as though her knees were going to buckle under her, but she did what he said, leading the mare back into the barn and refastening the lead rope. He was going to call the police! They were going to be arrested! What would their parents say?

Trembling, she returned to the yard.

The man's eyes narrowed as he looked back and forth between the girls and their ponies. "Stay right there!" he ordered, backing toward the door of the house with his gun still directed at them.

He's going in to call the police! Ashleigh thought, feeling faint.

The man kicked open the door, then hesitated. "I can't be bothered watching you till the cops get here," he muttered. "Get on those ponies and get off my land! And don't ever let me see you back here again!"

Both girls scrambled to the ponies and mounted before he could change his mind.

"If I catch you on my land again," he shouted, "I'll make good use of the buckshot in this gun!" He reinforced his threat by pointing the barrel of his gun in the air and firing.

Terrified by the noise, the ponies bolted off up the drive at a gallop, nearly unseating Ashleigh and Mona. Ashleigh almost expected to hear more shots cracking through the woods around them. The girls didn't slow down until they were far from the farmhouse, and only then for the ponies' sake. The drive was too rutted for such high speed.

Ashleigh's heart was pounding so hard that it echoed in her ears as she pulled Moe back into a trot. She looked over to Mona, whose face was white as a sheet.

"I've never been so scared," Mona said.

"Neither have I. I was sure we were going to be arrested."

"Or shot," Mona said. "I don't know which would have been worse. We should never have taken the mare out of the barn."

"I wasn't thinking of anything except helping her," Ashleigh said, mortified at what she'd done. Her heart had been in the right place, but she'd definitely been in the wrong. "Oh, Mona, I really didn't think of it as stealing a horse. I just felt so bad for that poor mare."

"So did I. I wasn't thinking, either. What if he called the police after we left? What would our parents say?"

Ashleigh shuddered. "I don't want to think about it. My father would skin me alive if he found out I tried to steal a horse."

"But we weren't really stealing her," Mona protested. "We were trying to save her."

"That's not what it would look like to the police. The man caught me red-handed leading her away. And . . . and if he hadn't caught me, I know I would have brought her back to Edgardale."

"Do they send kids off to reform school for something like this?" Mona asked, her voice trembling.

"I don't know, but I heard about a boy who was sent to one of those places for shoplifting."

"What are we going to do, Ash?" Mona asked. "Even if he doesn't call the police, we can't tell our parents what happened. But we have to tell them something."

"Well, we can tell them the truth," Ashleigh said. "We got lost. That wouldn't be a lie—we were lost even before we found the mare."

"You're right," Mona agreed, "but it still feels like a lie."

"I know." Ashleigh groaned and looked back over

her shoulder. She could almost feel the man's eyes boring into her back. "I wonder who he is. I don't remembering hearing anyone talk about a strange person living around here. Do you?"

"No. Maybe he's in hiding," Mona suggested, then shivered.

Ashleigh's hazel eyes popped wide open. "What do you mean? Like a bank robber or a murderer?"

"Maybe."

"No, Mona. If he was a criminal, he wouldn't have threatened to call the police."

"Maybe he was just trying to scare us."

"If he didn't want anyone to know where he is," Ashleigh said, "he wouldn't have let us go. We could identify him." That thought didn't make her feel any more comfortable.

"Right now I just want to get as far away from him as we can," Mona said. "I wish this road were better. I wish I knew where it led."

Ashleigh glanced up at the darkening sky. Never had Moe's brisk trot seemed so slow. The drive seemed to go on forever, and they weren't even sure where it would take them. She was beginning to feel like the woods were closing in on her when, suddenly, she saw brightness ahead and heard the hum of a car passing. "A road, Mona! We made it!"

As if sensing the girls' relief, the ponies trotted faster, then stopped when the drive met the shoulder of a two-lane highway. Another car sped by. Ashleigh looked up and down the road, trying to get her bearings.

"Do you recognize this?" she asked Mona.

Mona was frowning, deep in thought. Then she suddenly smiled. "Yes! This is the road to Meyersville. My mom comes this way when she visits one of her friends. But, boy, are we a long way from home. This way," she said, urging Silver to the left.

Ashleigh followed. She glanced back at the drive they'd just left. It was barely visible, without a sign or a mailbox marking the entrance. She shivered again, thinking of the poor, suffering horse trapped back there. *That horse is in more trouble than we are,* she thought sadly.

"How much farther do you think we have to go?" Ashleigh asked. She and Mona were riding so close together on the grassy shoulder of the road that their legs nearly touched. It was too dark for Ashleigh to see or recognize any landmarks.

Mona sounded as tired and cold as Ashleigh felt. "I think we're almost at the crossroad, and then we can take a shortcut to your place. I just wish I could call my parents."

The road they were following wound through a rural area bordered by woods and pastures, but few houses. The windows of those they passed were dark. Ashleigh didn't want to admit to herself how cold, hungry, and tired she was. If only they could find a welcoming house with lighted windows, so that she and Mona could call home!

Mom and Dad must be furious at me, Ashleigh thought. She was supposed to have been home hours ago to do her chores. But she was so tired, she didn't care if her parents were angry with her; she didn't care if they yelled. She just wanted to be home in her warm house, where there were good meals and lots of hugs.

"So do I." Ashleigh shivered as a cold breeze blew up under her sweatshirt. It was still April, after all, and the nights could get chilly, especially when you weren't dressed for it. "I know it's dark, Mona, but we have to try to go a little faster. The moon's coming up, and the ground is level. Moe is telling me that he wants to get home. Let's canter—at least until we hit rough ground again."

Ashleigh couldn't see Mona's nod, but she could sense it as her friend called to her pony, "Let's go home, Silv."

They were careful, looking ahead for any rough ground visible in the pale moonlight. The faster pace warmed them, but it sure didn't end their pangs of hunger or their worry over their parents' reactions.

"Mona, Mona," Ashleigh finally called. "I see lights up ahead. I recognize where we are now. Those are Edgardale's barn lights!" Ashleigh heeled Moe forward with new energy. "I can't wait to get home! I never thought I could get so lost in Kentucky. I don't even care if I get grounded for a month."

Mona laughed. "Neither do I!"

They galloped the ponies down the gravel drive. The ponies were obviously glad to be back in familiar surroundings, where there would be clean stalls with deep bedding, a bucket of grain, another of water, and a full hay net.

Ashleigh saw her mother standing in the yard with Mona's mom, Caroline, and Rory. They all turned at the sound of the ponies' clattering hooves. At first their expressions were uncertain, but then their faces lit with joy as they realized the riders were Ashleigh and Mona.

"Mom!" Ashleigh cried. "Mom, I'm sorry! We got lost."

"Thank God you're safe!" Mrs. Griffen ran to her daughter as Ashleigh pulled Moe to a stop. Mrs. Gardner came running, too.

"Mona!" she called. "You had us scared to death! Where have you been? What happened?"

Each woman drew her daughter into a tight embrace as soon as the girls dismounted. Caroline and Rory rushed over, full of questions.

"Dad and Mona's father are out looking for you," Rory said.

"Oh, Ash, I'm so glad you're okay," Caroline cried. "We were all so afraid. We thought you'd gotten hurt or something."

"We got lost—really lost." Words of explanation tumbled from Ashleigh's lips. "We were so scared, especially when it started getting dark. It's so good to be home!"

Ashleigh discovered there were tears in her eyes. Never had she appreciated her home and family so much.

Her mother was also blinking back tears, Ashleigh noticed. "You can tell us everything once we get you two inside. You're both freezing and probably starving, too. Caro, Rory, take care of the ponies, will you?" She put an arm around Ashleigh's shoulders.

Ashleigh looked up at her mother's face. "You're not mad at us?"

Her mother seemed surprised. "Mad? No, we're just so relieved you're all right."

Mrs. Gardner nodded her agreement and hugged Mona. "You're safe, and that's all that matters."

Ashleigh breathed a sigh of relief. Still, she couldn't stop herself from wondering what their mothers would say if they knew the girls had almost stolen a horse.

5

Ashleigh was walking through a dark, overgrown wilderness, lost and struggling to find her way. She heard the anguished cries of a horse in the distance. Then, at the far end of a pasture, she saw a shaggy white horse, nearly dead from starvation. She ran toward the horse, wanting to catch it and give it hay, but her body felt frozen. Her panic rose as the horse continued to cry out for help. Finally Ashleigh's legs began to move as if in slow motion, taking her toward the horse. Suddenly a man rose from the pasture grass and blocked her path. Ashleigh tried to go around him, but whichever way she turned, he was there, keeping her away from the horse. Her heart was beating so hard, she could barely catch her breath. If she didn't get past this man, the horse was going to die!

Ashleigh sat up in bed. Her forehead felt clammy from sweat. It had seemed so real. But it wasn't, she told herself. It was just a dream. She looked over at Caroline, sleeping soundly in her bed three feet away. She was home, in her own bed, and not out in the woods.

Still, the aftermath of the dream was so strong that Ashleigh couldn't go back to sleep. Her sheets were tangled from her tossing and turning. She glanced at her clock. Her alarm wouldn't go off for another half hour, but she decided to get up.

Careful not to disturb Caroline, she dressed and went out to the barn. The familiar, welcoming smells of horse, hay, and leather calmed her and brightened her spirits.

Most of the horses were still asleep, although she could hear Kurt somewhere in the back of the barn filling feed pails. She knew her parents would be out in a few minutes, too, but she needed this moment of early morning peace, just her and the horses.

She checked on Moe and saw that he was out like a light, obviously sleeping off his exertions of the day before. Kurt came into the barn with a quick "good morning" to Ashleigh. He rarely said more than that to anybody. Ashleigh knew he wasn't a cold man, despite his lack of conversation. He was just more comfortable around horses than people. He began leading the mares and foals out, and Ashleigh got to work on her chores.

She'd mucked out two stalls before her parents entered the barn. They both looked at her in surprise. "You didn't have to come out so early, sweetheart," her mother said.

"I couldn't sleep," Ashleigh answered quietly. "I wanted to be out with the horses."

Neither of them said anything. Ashleigh knew they understood. They both loved horses and found comfort in them, just as she did.

"I'm sorry about yesterday, Mom, Dad," Ashleigh began, feeling that she still owed them an explanation. They'd talked briefly the night before around the kitchen table, but Mona's parents had wanted to get her home, and Ashleigh had practically fallen asleep sitting up.

"Just don't go up there again," Ashleigh's father said. "Stay a little closer to home. I admire your spirit of adventure, but let's concentrate your energy down here in our paddocks." He chucked her chin affectionately. "I know you're going to do great things, Ashleigh, but have patience."

His words only made her feel more guilty. Doing great things didn't mean almost stealing someone's horse.

*　　*　　*

When Ashleigh got on the bus Monday morning, Mona greeted her with a serious expression.

"I dreamed about the mare last night," Mona said. "And the night before."

"You did?" Ashleigh exclaimed. "So did I. I dreamed that she was calling to me to help her, but I couldn't get to her because that awful man was in the way."

"Weird. I had practically the same dream."

"Not so weird." Ashleigh was silent for a moment. "We have to do something to help that horse."

"I know," Mona agreed, "but what can we do? If we tell our parents about her and they go over there, that man will tell them he caught us trying to take her."

"How about if we call one of the humane societies?"

"Do they help horses?" Mona asked. "I thought they only took care of dogs and cats."

Ashleigh thought about it. "Well, it wouldn't hurt to call and ask," she declared. "We have to do something."

"But would they even listen to us?" Mona asked. "Or believe us? We're just kids."

"I know, but I still think I should try," Ashleigh answered.

Mona chewed her lip nervously. "Okay, I guess. When do you want to do it?"

"Today," Ashleigh answered. "I'll call as soon as I get home from school."

Ashleigh hopped off the bus that afternoon and hurried down the drive, into the house, and up to her room. She wanted to use the phone before Caroline got home. She quickly changed out of her school clothes into a sweatshirt and jeans, then went to the kitchen to get the phone book. She took it into the den, where there was an extension, and flipped to the yellow pages. The book covered most of the county, since all of the nearby towns were so small.

What should I look under? she wondered. *Humane?*

The only headings there were for human services.

Okay, Ashleigh thought. *How about animal?*

She flipped to that and found a heading for animal shelters. Three were listed, all in neighboring towns. She chose the one closest to Edgardale and dialed.

After a couple of rings, a woman answered. "County Humane Society."

"Hello," Ashleigh replied, then hesitated, trying to frame her words. "Ah . . . I have a question. Do you do any work with horses?"

"Horses?" There was a pause. "What type of work? We certainly don't have any horses here."

53

"Do you rescue them, I mean?"

"You have a horse that you no longer want?" the woman asked, sounding confused.

"Oh, no, no," Ashleigh cried. "You see, my friend and I found a horse, but it's been neglected and half starved, and we want to save it."

"How old are you?" the woman asked cautiously.

Ashleigh was tempted to lie, but she didn't. "Ten."

"And have you told your parents about this horse?"

"Well, no," Ashleigh admitted. "It's on private property—somebody else's." Ashleigh wasn't sure just how much she should say. She didn't want to get into the fact that she'd taken the horse out of the barn without permission.

"I see. And have you approached the horse's owner?"

"Ah, no. I don't think he'd listen," Ashleigh said.

"I'm sorry, but I don't think we can help you. First of all, we rarely deal with large animals, and then only in exceptional circumstances. There are legalities to consider. The society can't go in and take an animal from its owner without very good evidence of mistreatment."

Ashleigh frowned. If the humane society couldn't take the mare from that awful man, who could?

"Second," the woman went on, "you should speak

to your parents about this horse and get their advice. Do they know anything about horses?"

"Yes, of course. We own a breeding farm."

"Then they would seem the perfect people to talk to. Or is there something you're not telling me? Is this horse in fact owned by your parents?"

"No! They would never treat a horse so badly."

"Then talk to them. If they agree that the animal's situation requires drastic action, then please have *them* call this office, and if we can't help, perhaps we can find someone who will. Can you give me your name and phone number?"

Ashleigh hung up in a panic. She could imagine her parents' reaction if this woman were to call them to verify Ashleigh's story when they knew nothing about the horse.

"Ash?" said a voice from the hall. Ashleigh jumped and turned around. Caroline was standing just outside the den, looking curiously at Ashleigh.

Ashleigh tried to keep her voice light. "Oh, hi, Caro."

Caroline wasn't deceived. "What are you doing making a call from in here? And what was that all about? Who's treating a horse badly?"

Ashleigh thought furiously. "Oh, I was just talking to Mona . . . about a story we were reading in school."

She could see from Caro's expression that she wasn't buying that explanation. Ashleigh just prayed Mona didn't walk into the house that second and show Ashleigh's explanation to be the fib it was.

But Caroline just shook her head. "Sometimes, Ash, I don't know about you. Do you have a secret boyfriend or something?"

"Me?" Ashleigh exclaimed.

Caroline laughed. "Right! That was a stupid suggestion. You'd rather spend time with a horse than with a boy!"

Ashleigh was about to shout back that there was nothing wrong with loving horses. It beat giggling on the phone for *hours* to your girlfriends. But Caroline had already turned, and Ashleigh didn't want to encourage any more questions from her sister.

She couldn't risk letting her parents find out about the mare.

6

Ashleigh raced out of the house as soon as she saw Mona pedaling down the drive. The ponies were still sore after their weekend adventure, so Mona had used her bike. The girls met in the parking area in front of the barn. Mona looked excited and curious. "Did you call?" she asked.

"Yes, but it wasn't good news, Mona. Let's go over and see the foals, and I'll tell you what happened."

Mona rested her bike against the side of the barn and followed Ashleigh along one of the grassy paths that led to the pastures. A few more mares and foals had been moved out of the juvenile paddock and were now grazing there, the mares keeping a watchful eye on their offspring. Ashleigh grinned as she watched the foals romping and playing with their fellow youngsters.

Ashleigh's favorites ran to the fence as soon as they saw her and Mona.

"They're looking for treats," Ashleigh told her friend. "I stashed some here the other day," she added, lifting the lid of a small watertight box that held extra lead shanks. She pulled out an apple and several carrots.

The young horses could only be fed small pieces, so Mona took a tiny bite from the apple, spit it out into her hand, and offered it to the foal. Ashleigh did likewise with the carrot. Soon other foals caught wind of the treat fest and started gamboling over.

"They're all so adorable!" Mona said with a sigh.

Ashleigh nodded. But even the babies couldn't cheer her up today. She kept thinking about the poor neglected mare, who never received such treats.

She told Mona about her phone call to the humane society.

Mona listened carefully. "It doesn't sound good, does it, Ash?"

"No," Ashleigh agreed. "I don't know what to do. I really want to talk to my parents about it, but I'm so afraid they'll be angry—not only because we almost stole the mare, but because we didn't tell them the whole truth that night."

"I know what you mean," Mona said. "But maybe we should tell our parents anyway. It might be worth getting in trouble if they could get help for the mare."

Ashleigh frowned. "But after talking to the lady at the humane society, I don't know if they could help, either. She said something about legal stuff, and that they couldn't just go in and take an animal away from its owner. Maybe our parents couldn't get past the legal stuff, either."

"You mean they could go up there, see how bad off the mare is, and still not be able to save her?" Mona asked.

"That's pretty much what the humane society lady said. Plus, if they did go up there, you know that nasty old man will tell them that we tried to take the mare."

"And then we'd be in big trouble. But he threatened to shoot us!" Mona exclaimed. "He should get in trouble for that!"

"If he knew our parents or the humane society people were coming, he wouldn't bring out his gun. And it's his word against ours. And we were trespassing. He may have already taken the mare away, or just left her there, tied in her stall without food or water."

"Don't say that, Ash!" Mona cried.

"I don't like to think about it, but if he's a murderer or a bank robber like you said, he wouldn't hang around for a horse."

Ashleigh was quiet for a moment, then spoke

earnestly. "We've got to take responsibility for her ourselves. Go check on her, bring her food, see if she's okay—at least until we can come up with another plan."

"That's what I was thinking, too. But could we find our way back there and home again without getting lost?" Mona asked.

"We've got to be better prepared this time. Dad has some orange tape in the tack room that he ties onto the horses during hunting season. Nobody would notice if I took some. We could tie it to branches so that we could find our way back."

"Sounds good to me," Mona said. "When do we go?"

"Tomorrow?" Ashleigh suggested. She was worried about the mare being left alone too long.

Mona considered, then nodded. "Okay, tomorrow. Silver and Moe should be better by then. Now let's get going on that homework!"

That night over dinner, Ashleigh's parents announced that they had a surprise for the family. Ashleigh looked up with interest. It wasn't often that her parents could afford a surprise.

"Do you want to tell them, or should I?" Mrs. Griffen asked her husband with a smile.

"Why don't you?" he replied, smiling, too.

This ought to be good, Ashleigh thought, waiting for her mother to continue.

"Well, we got a pleasant surprise in the mail today," Mrs. Griffen said. "You remember the Fontaines, who bought Wanderer's yearling from us two years ago?"

They all nodded. The Fontaines were memorable because they'd been such enthusiastic horse people and had fallen for Wanderer's yearling like a ton of bricks. The yearling was memorable, too. She'd been the star of the foal crop that year—a spunky, intelligent black filly with perfect conformation. Ashleigh remembered chasing around the paddocks with her in a game of tag the filly always won. She'd missed the filly badly when the Fontaines had bought her.

"They named her Wanderer's Quest," Ashleigh said, remembering.

"Right, and she's running on the undercard on Derby day," Mrs. Griffen said. "Your father and I have been following her. She had a late start, but she's been doing very well this year, and looks to have a good chance of winning her race."

"But what's the surprise?" Rory demanded.

Mrs. Griffen laughed. "Well, in thanks for raising such a talented racehorse, the Fontaines have invited us to watch the whole day's races from their box."

"They've invited us to the Kentucky Derby?" Ashleigh exclaimed excitedly.

"Indeed they have," Mr. Griffen confirmed. "And you know how hard—if not impossible—it is to get clubhouse seats on Derby day."

Ashleigh nearly jumped out of her seat, then remembered her manners. "We're going to the Derby! I can't wait to tell Mona. I don't suppose I could invite her . . . ?"

Mr. Griffen shook his head. "Sorry, but they've invited only us."

Rory was equally as excited as Ashleigh. He loved the races, even if he didn't understand the intricacies of who won or lost. He just liked to see the horses speeding around the track. Even Caroline, who wasn't much of a racing enthusiast, looked pleased. Going to the Derby would give her a chance to dress up like a model. Ashleigh imagined her sister was already thinking about what outfit to wear, and of course she'd need a hat. Everyone wore hats to the Derby.

"It goes without saying," Mrs. Griffen said in mock seriousness, "that we'll expect you all to be on your best behavior until Derby day. No missed chores." She turned to Ashleigh. "No missed homework assignments." Ashleigh flushed. "And if you want us to place any bets for you, it will have to come out of your allowance money."

They all nodded. Ashleigh was good at saving for special riding equipment she wanted, while Caroline tended to spend most of her extra money on clothes. But placing bets on their favorite horses was the least important part of going to the Derby. Ashleigh was already dreaming about backside tours, meeting trainers and jockeys and seeing the magnificent horses firsthand.

Before Ashleigh went out to the barn to bid the horses good night, she called Mona.

"You won't believe this!" she told her friend breathlessly.

"What?" Mona cried. "Has something happened?"

"Something really good," Ashleigh answered, dragging out the suspense. "I'm going to the Kentucky Derby! My whole family, that is. We'll be sitting in the clubhouse. Do you believe it?"

Mona was silent for a second. "Oh, Ash, you're so lucky! Wow, clubhouse seats for the Derby. You'll be able to see everything from up there!"

"I know. I almost feel like pinching myself to make sure I'm not dreaming."

"But how?" Mona asked. "Did your parents buy tickets? How did they even find any?"

Ashleigh quickly explained.

"I remember Wanderer's Quest. She was a real beauty, even as a yearling. So what race is she running in?" Mona asked.

"I was so excited I didn't even ask," Ashleigh said, "but I'll find out and tell you all about it tomorrow."

"Are we still riding up to check on the mare tomorrow afternoon?" Mona asked.

"Yes," Ashleigh said, sobering. "The Derby news is exciting, but I keep thinking about that poor horse. Imagine what she would look like if she were well fed and groomed, especially with her conformation. Like white lightning."

"That's what we should call her, Ash!" Mona exclaimed. "Lightning. She needs a name."

"You're right," Ashleigh answered thoughtfully. "Wouldn't it be neat if someday she was fit enough to run like lightning?"

"Right now she looks too weak to run at all," Mona said sadly.

"Well, we're going to help her," Ashleigh declared. "Starting tomorrow."

After she hung up, Ashleigh hurried out to the barn. She found her mother in the tack room. "Mom, I forgot to ask. What race is Wanderer's Quest running in?"

Mrs. Griffen sorted through a pile of blankets, pulling out those that needed to be cleaned. "The Providian Mile," she answered, "a turf race for fillies and mares age three and up."

"A turf race? Wanderer never ran on the grass."

"No, but Quest's sire has some grass runners in his pedigree, and apparently the filly has done her best work on the grass. She won her last race at Gulfstream impressively. The Fontaines decided it was enough to justify entering her in stakes company."

"It'll be good news for Edgardale if she wins," Ashleigh said.

"It sure will. It's always good news for us when one of our foals goes on to success and attracts the attention of new clients."

"Can I borrow your *Daily Racing Form?*"

Mrs. Griffen laughed. "It's in the office. Is your homework done?"

"Yup," Ashleigh said as she hurried off.

"All right, but I don't want you reading till all hours of the night."

"I promise," Ashleigh called back over her shoulder. "I just can't believe one of our babies is going to be running on Derby day. Wanderer must be so proud!"

*   *   *

About seven that night, Kurt banged on the back door with bad news. Wanderer was acting strange.

"Wanderer?" Ashleigh cried, looking up from the back issues of the *Daily Racing Form* she was reading at the kitchen table. Wanderer sick, when only a few hours ago they had been talking about watching one of her foals run?

Ashleigh jumped up and followed her parents and Rory out the back door. Caroline was upstairs on the phone and hadn't heard Kurt's alarming message.

Wanderer, the beautiful black mare who had produced some of the best foals for the farm, was grunting in discomfort when they reached her stall. Kurt opened the stall door, and Elaine and Derek Griffen hurried in. Wanderer's foal, a little colt they called Tonka, huddled in the corner of the big box stall, frightened by his mother's distress.

The elder Griffens went to the mare's side. "Ashleigh and Rory, can you take care of the foal?" Mr. Griffen asked. "Bring him out into the aisle while we take a look at Wanderer."

Ashleigh quickly grabbed a lead and the foal's tiny halter. Tonka didn't protest as they put on his halter, but when they tried to lead him out of the stall, he squealed and balked. He had no intention of leaving his mother.

"Rory," Ashleigh said, "put your arm around the foal's hindquarters and push while I pull on the lead."

The foal continued to squeal his protests, but they managed to get him out of the stall and into the aisle, where they both cuddled and tried to reassure him.

"What do you think, Rory?" Ashleigh whispered. "Colic?"

Rory solemnly nodded his agreement. Young as they were, they had learned firsthand about the diseases and injuries that could afflict the horses in their parents' charge. Colic was an intestinal disorder usually caused by something the horse had eaten. It could also be caused by the horse eating too much rich grain. And it could lead to death.

"Let's get her out and walking," Ashleigh heard her father say. "Kurt, give the vet a call. I think we might need him. It looks like colic, but I hope we've caught it in time. At least she hasn't started rolling yet."

Ashleigh and Rory held on tightly to the foal as Mr. Griffen led his dam out of the stall. They knew the foal would struggle to follow her.

When Mr. Griffen had led Wanderer far up the aisle, Mrs. Griffen told Ashleigh and Rory to take the foal back into the stall and stay with him.

Although they couldn't see what was going on outside the closed stall door, they could hear the clatter of Wanderer's shod hooves as their parents led her up and down the concrete aisle. They could also hear the worried tone in their parents' hushed voices. A few minutes later the vet arrived, and they brought the mare to the isolation stall at the end of the barn so he could examine her.

The foal had quieted at last, comforted by their warm bodies as they cradled him. At first Ashleigh had been able to feel his heart pounding with fear, but eventually his heartbeat slowed to normal. He gave a little grunting sigh, then closed his eyes in sleep.

"That's it, Tonka," Rory whispered. "You go to sleep. We'll take good care of you."

Despite her worry, Ashleigh smiled at her brother. In all the commotion, she'd almost forgotten that Rory had named Wanderer's foal after his favorite toy trucks.

Not long after, the vet and Mr. Griffen came back down the aisle. Ashleigh strained to hear what they were talking about and thought she heard them say, ". . . caught it in time." She hoped she'd heard right.

Rory, she noticed, had laid his tousled head down on the foal's rump and was fast asleep. Still cradling the foal's head, Ashleigh leaned back against the stall wall. She had no intention of falling asleep until she found out if Wanderer was all right.

The next thing she knew, she felt a hand on her shoulder. She heard her mother's voice. "Ash, honey? Wake up, sweetheart. Wanderer's going to be okay, we think."

Ashleigh forced her eyes open and saw her mother kneeling in the stall beside her. She shook her head and rubbed her eyes. "I didn't fall asleep. I was just resting."

Her mother smiled. "It's late. Your father's already carried Rory inside, but you're getting too big to carry."

"Who's going to stay with the foal?" Ashleigh asked in alarm.

"Kurt will."

"And Wanderer?"

"Your father and I will be out here until we're sure she's going to be okay. You need your sleep. You have school tomorrow."

School, Ashleigh thought. *Why do I have to go to school when there's so much happening on the farm?*

Kurt came into the stall, his expression one of concern. He had a horse blanket with him, which he gently draped over the sleeping foal. The foal stirred as Ashleigh moved his head off her lap, but he didn't wake. Her mother helped her to her feet. Ashleigh's legs were cramped from sitting cross-legged for so long.

"I'll take good care of him," Kurt told Ashleigh. He wasn't one for words, but he loved the horses.

Mrs. Griffen walked Ashleigh back to the house. She kissed Ashleigh's cheek. "Don't worry, sweetheart. Everything's going to be all right."

Ashleigh stumbled up the stairs to her room. Caroline was sound asleep. Too tired to change into her pajamas, Ashleigh crawled into bed and pulled the covers over her. Her last thoughts were of Wanderer and her foal—and of another mare who wasn't getting any caring attention at all.

First thing the next morning, Ashleigh rushed out to the stable. She didn't even stop to eat breakfast. Neither her mother nor father was in the kitchen, although a sleepy Caroline was.

"Where are you going in such a hurry?" Caroline asked as she took a cereal box from the cupboard.

"To see how Wanderer is, of course!" Ashleigh shot back. "Not that you care that our best broodmare might have died during the night!"

"Of course I care, Ashleigh Griffen," Caroline

answered angrily. "I just don't see what good it would do for me to hang around the stable. Mom and Dad know what they're doing."

Ashleigh snorted, then slammed through the door. Her mother, looking exhausted, was coming out of the barn as Ashleigh dashed up. Ashleigh immediately thought the worst, but her mother smiled.

"It's going to be okay, sweetie," she said. "Wanderer has pulled through. In fact, she's almost her old self. She couldn't wait to get back to her foal."

Ashleigh threw her arms around her mother's waist. "Oh, Mom, I'm so glad! I know how important Wanderer is to the farm."

Her mother returned the hug, then said with a touch of humor, "I see you slept in your clothes. I know, you were too tired to change into your pj's. Just make sure you change before you head out to school. Go on in and see Wanderer. What I need right now is a strong cup of coffee."

Ashleigh hurried into the stable. Most of the mares had their heads over the half doors, waiting to be taken outside after their morning meal. Ashleigh called individual good mornings to them, then stopped outside Wanderer's stall and looked in. The black mare was nuzzling her foal, obviously glad to be reunited with him.

"How're you feeling, girl?" Ashleigh asked softly. "Better?"

The mare whickered and returned her attention to her foal.

"Guess that's a yes," Ashleigh said with a smile.

Mr. Griffen strode down the aisle from his office at the end. "You're up early, young lady," he said.

"I was worried about Wanderer."

"She's going to be fine, thank heavens, though it was touch and go for a while there. As long as you're here, how about giving me and Kurt a hand taking the horses out? Your mother is exhausted."

"You must be, too."

Her father smiled wearily. "Well, yes, but it's all part of the job. We knew what we were getting into when we decided to start a breeding farm. Why don't you get Jolita and her foal? She's easy to handle. I'll get Georgie, our troublemaker."

A half hour later, Ashleigh and her father had finished bringing out the mares and foals, with the exception of Wanderer, who would stay in her stall that day so they could keep an eye on her progress. By then, Caroline and Rory had arrived to do their morning chores.

Caroline walked over to Ashleigh. "I'll do half your stalls for you," she offered.

Ashleigh looked at her sister in amazement. "You will?"

"Yeah. You worked hard enough last night." Although Caroline's tone was breezy. Ashleigh wondered if her sister wasn't feeling a little bit guilty. "Mom wants you up for breakfast, anyway."

Ashleigh's lips twitched, but she managed to hide her smile. "Well, thanks, Caro."

Ashleigh was ready when Mona arrived on Silver after school. She'd stored a roll of orange tape in her backpack. The tape was easy to rip, so she didn't need scissors. She'd also filled a bag with half a dozen scoops of vitamin-enhanced horse feed. Her parents often gave the feed to nursing mares to keep them in top health, so Ashleigh figured it would also be good for a malnourished animal like Lightning. She'd worn her watch, too. She wasn't about to take any chances on getting back late.

The day was overcast, but it didn't look like rain. The air was spring-scented as the girls headed the ponies up toward the woods.

"Are you sure we can find our way back to Lightning's barn?" Mona asked.

"No," Ashleigh replied honestly. "But it hasn't rained since we were here Saturday, so I'm hoping we can still see our tracks and follow them."

"And this time we're going to be more careful about marking our trail," Mona teased.

"You bet we are! I've got the tape in my backpack. I'll mark every tree along the way if I have to." They both chuckled, even though they knew their mission was deadly serious.

The trip up to the spring-fed stream was easy, and so was the next stretch of the deer trail—until it split into two separate paths. Ashleigh dismounted and studied the ground. She found several faint hoof-prints. "This way," she said, pointing to the right and getting the tape out of her pack. She tore off several pieces and tied them securely to the tree branches on either side of the trail. "I'll tie on some more a little farther down," she told Mona as she mounted again, and they set off.

Ashleigh continued marking the trail as they wound through the woods. At this point the trail worked its way steadily uphill, but soon they reached another fork. Again Ashleigh dismounted, but the ground was harder here, and the ponies had left no tracks. Ashleigh groaned. Then she noticed the broken branch at the end of the left-hand path. It was one of the marks she'd left during their original trip, before she'd forgotten to leave markers. She reinforced that marker with her orange tape, and they continued on.

They only had to guess about their path once, choosing the trail leading downhill rather than up. Luck was with them, because soon they recognized the wooded landscape leading to the back of the run-down farm.

"I'm nervous," Mona whispered. "What if he's here?"

"We'll just have to be really careful and check everything out before we leave the woods," Ashleigh whispered back.

The clearing was just ahead. They stopped the ponies while they were still hidden by the trees and looked down at the dilapidated buildings and grounds.

Ashleigh immediately noticed that Lightning was in the small pasture behind the barn—not that there was anything for her to graze on but weeds. She looked no worse than the last time they'd seen her, but certainly no better, either. Still, Ashleigh felt a wave of relief just knowing the mare was still there and still alive. She saw the same relief on Mona's face.

Neither of them spoke, but Lightning must have scented them or the ponies. She slowly lifted her head and looked toward the woods. Just then her owner came around the corner of the barn with a light harness in his hand. The mare quickly turned her head toward him, and Ashleigh could almost see the poor horse retreat into herself, cringing away from him, even though she didn't move.

The man threw open the rickety pasture gate and approached the horse. He grabbed her halter, then quickly secured the harness over her bony shoulders.

"You got it easy today," he said roughly to the mare. "You only got one engine block to load. Do a good job and I might give you some hay tonight instead of leaving you in the pasture."

Ashleigh and Mona exchanged glances and frowned.

An engine block? Ashleigh wondered. *Does this guy sell used auto parts? Is that why there are so many junked cars all over the place?* She continued watching as the man led Lightning out of the crude pasture and around the side of the barn. They reappeared in back of the farmhouse. Ashleigh now noticed a battered pickup truck parked near the edge of the junk-filled yard. Behind it was a tall iron tripod fitted with heavy chains. The man attached Lightning's harness to two of the chains, which ran over pulleys at the top of the tripod. Those chains, in turn, were wrapped around something on the ground.

Ashleigh didn't understand exactly what Mr. Nasty was doing until he led Lightning forward, and the chains connected to her harness tightened. He forcefully urged the mare on again, and she struggled another few steps forward. Slowly a black rectangular object, which Ashleigh assumed was the engine block Mr. Nasty had talked about, rose in the air behind the truck.

"He's using a block and tackle to lift things," Mona said. "Incredibly heavy things that he could never lift himself. The pulleys help offset some of the weight, but it's still got to be a hard job for Lightning."

"Get on!" the man shouted to the mare, smacking her rump with a whip.

Mona reached over and laid a hand on Ashleigh's arm as they watched the poor mare try to move forward against the weight she was lifting. The mare was shaking with the effort, but the man showed no sympathy. He smacked her rump again, harder this time. The mare made a valiant effort, stepping once more into the harness and nearly going down on her knees. The engine block rose higher in the air.

"Stand!" the man then ordered. He jumped into the pickup and backed it up a few feet until the engine block was directly above the truck's bed. He stopped the truck, then went to the mare's head.

"Back!" he shouted, taking her halter. The mare took a step backward, then another. The man kept his eye on the engine block as it slowly inched down onto the truck bed. He continued backing the mare until the block of metal landed with a thump. Only then did he release the mare's halter.

She trembled and dropped her head, exhausted from the exertion. The man released the chains from her harness, then removed her harness as well.

Lightning stood unmoving, head down, totally drained and defeated, but the man offered her no kind words of thanks for her efforts. He began leading her back to the pasture. Ashleigh wondered if he would keep his word and give Lightning the hay she so obviously needed, but when he reappeared around the side of the barn, he had nothing in his hands. He put the mare in the pasture, closed the gate, and walked away. A few moments later he got in his truck, started the engine, and rumbled off down the drive.

Ashleigh watched the disappearing truck, then turned to Mona. "Let's go help her," she said. "We'd better move fast in case he comes back."

"He didn't even leave her water!" Mona said angrily as they heeled the ponies down the hill toward Lightning's pasture. The mare was so dispirited that she didn't even look up at their approach. Moe and

Silver both quietly whinnied, but Lightning did no more than twitch an ear back.

"I feel like crying," Ashleigh said. "How could anyone be so cruel?"

"At least we know now why he keeps her. He works her to the bone," Mona said. "I could strangle him with my bare hands for treating her like this."

"First let's give her some feed and water. Do you think he'll notice?"

Mona gave a snort of disgust. "I doubt he'll even come back to check on her."

They dismounted near the pasture gate and loosely tied the ponies' reins to the fence. Ashleigh removed her backpack. Mona found an empty water bucket in the corner of the pasture and went in search of a water source.

Ashleigh walked toward Lightning. The mare didn't even seem aware of her presence. Ashleigh spoke quietly and soothingly.

"Hi there, girl. I'm your friend, and so is Mona. We hate seeing you treated so badly. We want to help."

Still no response from Lightning.

Ashleigh rubbed a gentle hand down Lightning's neck and over her bony back. The mare's muscles twitched, but otherwise she didn't respond. Carefully Ashleigh examined her more thoroughly, checking her shaggy coat for hidden sores. She also inspected the horse's feet, which, though cracked and in need of a hoof trim, weren't in as poor condition as Ashleigh had initially feared. No doubt the exercise she got lifting heavy loads had kept the wall of her hoof from growing too long. Ashleigh gently lifted the mare's upper lip and checked her teeth. They needed filing, but Lightning didn't appear to be a terribly old animal—maybe ten or twelve, Ashleigh guessed.

Overall, Lightning seemed to be suffering more from overwork and poor nutrition—semistarvation was more like it—than any serious physical problems. But Ashleigh knew from watching her parents and the vets who came to Edgardale that there could be other, less visible problems, like parasites and anemia.

Mona returned with a full pail of water. "I found a hand pump next to the barn," she explained. "The water looks clean." She set the bucket down in front of Lightning's nose. The mare sniffed, then dipped her nose into the cool water and slowly drank.

"Whew!" Ashleigh and Mona said in unison.

"I wonder if I can get her to eat anything," Ashleigh mused. "I'm afraid to give her too much. She could get sick."

"Try a handful and see if she takes it," Mona suggested.

Ashleigh took the paper bag of feed from her backpack, scooped up some feed, and held her cupped hand under the mare's mouth.

The drink of water seemed to have revived Lightning a little. Now she lipped up a small portion of feed and chewed. Ashleigh kept her hand extended, and eventually the mare ate a little bit more. They continued this slow process until Lightning had finished two handfuls.

"I don't think I should give her any more," Ashleigh said worriedly. "When a horse hasn't eaten grain in a long time, too much can give them colic. What about hay? Do we dare sneak in and take some from the barn?"

"I don't think Mr. Nasty will be back yet," Mona said. "I'll go check, although it's probably not very good hay."

"It's got to be better than the weeds out here."

"Okay," Mona said. "I'll go, and you keep watch for Mr. Nasty."

As Mona set off, Ashleigh continued to rub Lightning, trying to show the mare through her light touch that she was a friend. Maybe it was Ashleigh's imagination, but Lightning did seem a little less despondent. Of course, Ashleigh knew that would change quickly when the man came back and continued his abuse.

She was glad to see Lightning dip her muzzle into the bucket and drink again—a good sign, Ashleigh knew, since the mare was probably dehydrated, too.

Mona returned with an armful of hay. "It's not a whole lot," she said, "but I didn't want to take so much that Mr. Nasty would notice."

Ashleigh checked her watch. She hated to leave Lightning, but she couldn't risk getting home late. "Mona, I was thinking. We can't leave the hay and feed where Mr. Nasty will see it and know someone's been here. Where did you find her water bucket?"

"In the corner of the pasture above the gate."

"Okay, let's leave the food a little farther away, so that if he comes to fill the bucket, he won't see it."

"If he even bothers to check the bucket," Mona said tersely.

"We'll leave it full, but she'll probably drink most of it before he gets back. I'll bring the feed and hay over, if you don't mind refilling the bucket."

Mona nodded. "I wish we could spend more time with her."

"Me too," Ashleigh agreed as she picked up her backpack and the hay Mona had brought. She headed toward the fence at the top of the pasture—which wasn't all that far away, since the pasture was so small.

"Come on, Lightning," she called quietly over her

shoulder. "Come on, sweetie. I'm going to put your food up here where it will be safe."

For a long moment the mare just stared after Ashleigh. Then she started walking slowly in Ashleigh's direction. Ashleigh wanted to cheer. It wasn't much of a response, but it was a start at building trust.

Ashleigh spread the hay behind some tall stalks of last year's dead weeds. Then she poured some feed on the ground beside it. She wished there were a place where she could stash the extra, but she knew the raccoons and other animals would find it. She'd just have to carry it home with her.

Mona returned with a full pail of water and set it in the packed dirt corner of the pasture where she'd found it, then she joined Ashleigh at Lightning's side. She patted the mare, too, and cooed to her. Ashleigh knew Mona was experiencing the same feelings that she was. They were such good friends that most of the time they could sense each other's feelings without having to say a word.

"You poor baby," Mona murmured, laying her cheek against Lightning's neck. "But don't worry. Somehow we're going to save you."

Moe suddenly gave an impatient whinny. Both girls looked up. They'd almost forgotten the ponies in their concentration on Lightning.

"Okay, Moe," Ashleigh called. "We're coming." She checked her watch again, then said to Mona, "We'd better go, or we'll be late."

Mona nodded and gave Lightning one final pat.

Ashleigh picked up her backpack and gave Lightning a long last look. "Go on, girl, eat. You need it. We'll be back—we promise."

As they left the pasture, Ashleigh glanced over her shoulder. Lightning had lowered her head and was plucking up mouthfuls of hay.

The girls carefully closed and refastened the gate and hurried to the ponies. "Sorry, Moe," Ashleigh apologized, "but she needs our help. She doesn't have a nice warm stall and a kind owner to take care of her."

Moe just snorted, anxious to get home to that warm stall. The girls mounted and trotted back to the path leading into the woods. They looked back before they disappeared into the leafy greenery. Lightning had lifted her head and was watching them. They each blew her a kiss and smiled.

"Step one," Ashleigh said.

Mona nodded happily. "I feel much better about her now. But we still haven't figured out how we're going to save her from Mr. Nasty."

"I know." Ashleigh frowned in thought. "But at

least we can keep checking on her and bringing her food."

Thanks to the orange tape, they easily found their way back to Edgardale before Ashleigh was due to start her evening chores. No one suspected they'd been up to anything. In fact, both of Ashleigh's parents smiled and waved as the girls rode in.

"I'm going to head straight home," Mona said. "I'll call you later. And don't forget your homework!"

Ashleigh grinned. "What are you, my third parent? But I won't forget it. I want to go to the Derby."

The girls waved goodbye to each other, and Ashleigh dismounted, untacked Moe, and took him to his stall. After she'd put his tack away, she went to visit Wanderer. The mare was looking much better.

"Maybe you'll be able to go out to the paddock tomorrow, sweetie," Ashleigh said. "I'll bet you'll be glad to get out of this stall."

Wanderer nickered and bobbed her head, as if she understood. Ashleigh chuckled, then went to help her parents check that the hay nets and water buckets were full. She had the same four stalls to oversee that she was charged with mucking out in the morning. Rory and Caroline were at work, too, though Ashleigh could see that Caroline resented the time away from her phone.

Ashleigh was conscientious that night about getting her homework done. She didn't even glance at the copies of the *Daily Racing Form* stacked beside her bed. In fact, the Derby was no longer uppermost on her mind. She couldn't stop thinking about Lightning and wondering what she and Mona could do to rescue her.

At lunch the next day Ashleigh noticed that Mona seemed especially quiet. Since Lynne and Jamie were off on an all-day science field trip, Ashleigh and Mona were sitting alone at their usual table in the cafeteria.

"I'd rather be on the field trip with Lynne and Jamie than here," Ashleigh said, hoping to start some kind of conversation with her friend.

"Mmm," Mona answered, as if she hadn't heard a word Ashleigh said.

Ashleigh raised her voice. Despite the cafeteria monitors keeping an eye on the place, other kids were shouting and holding loud conversations. Maybe Mona hadn't heard her.

Ashleigh repeated her comment.

"Oh, I heard you, Ash," Mona replied. "You'd rather be on the field trip. I don't blame you, but I was thinking about something else."

For perhaps the first time ever, Ashleigh could get no clue to what her friend was thinking. "What's wrong?" she asked.

Mona shook her head. "I had such bad dreams again last night—about Lightning."

"I had bad dreams, too," Ashleigh replied. "It was like I was living through everything that happened yesterday over and over again, but some of the stuff didn't make sense." Ashleigh wagged her head.

"Did you feel like, no matter how hard we tried to save Lightning, something bad happened?" Mona asked.

Ashleigh nodded. "Something like that."

"If you go up this afternoon with feed," Mona added, "I can't go with you—not because of my dreams," she quickly clarified. "But my mom reminded me last night that I have a dentist appointment after school." Mona glanced over to Ashleigh. "I'm sorry. I'm really not backing out on saving Lightning. I love her."

"It's okay, Mona," Ashleigh said. "I'm going to try to pack half a bale of hay on Moe's back, so at least Lightning will have something. I wasn't planning on staying long, anyway."

"Are you sure you want to go alone?" Mona asked nervously.

"Well, I'll probably be a little scared, but I'll be

careful and stay hidden until I'm sure Mr. Nasty's not around."

"If you go again later in the week, I'll go," Mona said. "I promise."

After school, Ashleigh changed into jeans and riding boots. She was trying to figure out how to fasten a bundle of hay to the back of Moe's saddle without anyone noticing. She hated to sneak around, but it was so important to help Lightning. As she walked into the kitchen, her mother was hurrying in through the back door.

"Ashleigh, good, you're home," Mrs. Griffen said with relief. "I just got a call from the school. Rory's taken a bad fall in the playground. They think he may have broken his arm. The ambulance has taken him to the hospital. I told them I'd meet them there."

"How did he fall?" Ashleigh exclaimed.

"I don't know. I didn't think to ask, I was so worried. I don't know how long we'll be gone. Your father and Kurt are going to need some extra help without me here. Will you give them a hand, sweetie?"

"Of course," Ashleigh said.

"Thanks. I'll call everyone from the hospital and let you know how Rory is."

Mrs. Griffen grabbed her purse and car keys from the counter and hurried back out the door. Ashleigh stood in the center of the kitchen for a moment. *I guess I won't be able to go see Lightning today,* she thought. But the mare had made it without their help until now. Ashleigh just prayed Lightning would be all right for another day.

I'll be there tomorrow, Lightning, Ashleigh silently promised. *I won't let you down.*

Then she headed out to the barn to help her father.

8

They didn't hear from Mrs. Griffen until close to six. By then Ashleigh could tell her father was getting worried. So was she. What was wrong with Rory that it was taking so long?

Caroline, reading the note Ashleigh had left on the kitchen table, came out to the barn as soon as she was dropped off by one of her friends' mothers. She'd had a club meeting after school. Without complaint, Caroline pitched in. That was one thing about her family, Ashleigh realized. They might sometimes disagree, but when there was trouble, they worked together like a unit.

When the stable office phone finally rang, Mr. Griffen sprinted off to answer it. Ashleigh and Caroline followed and listened as he picked up the receiver.

"Elaine!" he said breathlessly into the phone. "I was

worried sick. How is he? . . . Yes . . . Yes, I know the emergency room can be slow. What did the doctors say?" He frowned. "Uh-huh. Is he in pain?"

Ashleigh wished she could hear what her mother was saying. Was Rory all right? She and Caroline exchanged a nervous look.

"Okay," Mr. Griffen finally said. "Give him a big hug from me and tell him I love him. I love you, too." He hung up the phone and for a few seconds stood staring at the office wall.

"Dad!" Ashleigh and Caroline cried in unison. "What's happened? How is Rory?"

He quickly shook his head, then turned to them. "Sorry, girls. I know you're as worried as I am. Rory's going to be fine, but he has a compound fracture, so it was a little more serious than we initially thought. It took a while for the X rays to be processed. Then his arm had to be set. From what your mother said, I guess he's kind of sore. He scraped his face up pretty badly, too."

"How did his face get scraped?" Ashleigh asked. "What happened?"

Caroline looked alarmed. "He didn't get beat up or anything, did he?"

"No, nothing like that," Mr. Griffen said. "He fell off the jungle gym. He was trying to walk along the top of the monkey bars—I guess he was showing off—and he lost his balance and fell. The playground is mulched, but he landed on his arm and the side of his face, and from that height, even mulch can hurt."

Ashleigh breathed a sigh of relief. "Well, I guess we should get back to work," she said.

"Right," her dad agreed with a smile. "We want everything done so we can be with Rory when he gets home."

He led the way back into the barn. Ashleigh spent the rest of the evening filling hay nets, checking water buckets for the night, and taking a look in on the mares and their foals to make sure everyone was all right.

Kurt had worked with the family throughout, characteristically silent, except when he talked to the horses. There was only one mare left who hadn't foaled. Impish Gal had had delivery problems in the past, so Kurt had brought a cot down from his upstairs apartment over the rear of the barn. He began setting it up in the aisle next to her stall.

"Kurt, you don't have to sleep down here," Mr. Griffen exclaimed. "Impish isn't due till next week."

"I don't mind. You never know how close the mares will be to schedule, and you've got enough going on with your family tonight," Kurt said.

"Well, thanks, Kurt," Mr. Griffen said gratefully. "I *am* concerned about my son."

"No problem."

Caroline had gone up to the house a few minutes before to make sandwiches. Feeling tired, Ashleigh and her father headed that way, too. "Thanks for your help, Ash," her father said.

"You're welcome, and you know I don't mind." Ashleigh suddenly had a terrible thought. "But I didn't get my homework done. I didn't even start it!"

"Don't worry. It wasn't your fault, and I'll be glad to give you a hand."

Ashleigh looked up at her father and smiled. "Are you sure *you* remember how to do math?" she teased.

He chuckled. "I'm probably a little rusty," he admitted. "So it will be good for both of us."

Ashleigh helped Caroline set the table while they waited for their mother and Rory to arrive home. "I bet Rory will be feeling pretty rotten," Ashleigh said.

Caroline nodded. "They've been at the hospital a long time." She paused. "I think I hear the car."

Ashleigh hurried to the front door and peered out the window. "They're home! Mom will probably need help."

Caroline hurried outside, and Ashleigh unwrapped the plate of sandwiches and set it on the table. She looked up as Rory appeared, supported by Caro's arm. His normally bright face was marred on one side by deep scratches, and the rest of his face seemed pale.

Mr. Griffen came in from the hall and rushed over to his son. "How're you doing, little guy?" he asked.

"I hurt my arm," Rory said.

"I know. Come on, I'll give you a lift to the couch. You'll be more comfortable there." He lifted Rory in his arms, carried him into the living room, and laid him on the couch with a pillow behind his head. The rest of the family followed. Ashleigh and Caroline knelt down beside Rory and asked him all about the hospital and the huge plaster cast on his arm. Their parents conferred behind them.

"Can I get you anything?" Ashleigh asked. "Caro made sandwiches. You must be hungry."

"Kind of," Rory replied weakly.

"I'll fix you a plate," Ashleigh said, rising.

"Can you bring me some juice, too? Fruit punch."

"Sure."

Meanwhile, Caroline had collected more pillows to put behind Rory's back and a throw from the couch to put over his legs. "Warm enough?" she asked.

Rory nodded, then groaned. "I think I need a pillow under my cast."

"Sure." Caroline quickly eased one into place as Ashleigh came back into the room carrying a plate and Rory's favorite plastic cup filled with juice. She set them on the coffee table within Rory's reach.

"Anything else?" Ashleigh asked.

Rory gazed at his sisters with the soulful look of a hurt puppy. "Maybe a movie."

Ashleigh glanced at her parents, who had been listening. Normally they weren't allowed to watch TV or movies until after dinner was over and all homework was done. Of course, Rory didn't have homework in kindergarten. Her parents nodded, both with small, knowing smiles on their faces.

"The rest of you must be starved," Mrs. Griffen said. "I know I am. Rory, you'll be all right while we eat, won't you?"

"Can't you all come in here and eat?" Rory asked plaintively.

"You'll be fine," his mother assured him. "You broke your left arm, not your right, so you can eat. We'll be back in as soon as we're done."

Ashleigh gave her mother a puzzled look. Why would she leave Rory alone?

Mrs. Griffen winked and motioned Ashleigh and Caroline to the kitchen. Once there, out of Rory's earshot, their mother quickly explained. "If we don't want a little tyrant on our hands for the next few weeks, we're going to have stop catering to his every whim." She smiled. "I got the full treatment in the hospital and especially on the way home, 'Mommy, now that I'm so hurt, don't you think you and Daddy should get me that Tonka backhoe I wanted—and tell Ashleigh to let me ride Moe when I'm better?' He's playing it to the hilt. I think we have a budding actor in the family."

"But, Elaine," Mr. Griffen interrupted, "he *is* hurt."

"The doctors said he should be back on his feet by tomorrow. And all we have to do is make sure he doesn't do anything that will further injure his arm."

Ashleigh giggled and looked over to Caroline. "He had us snowed, Caro. We were waiting on him hand and foot."

Caro's eyes flashed. "And we would have kept doing it."

Their mother interrupted. "Rory does need some special attention, girls, especially for the next few days. But you don't need to be his servants."

Both girls burst into laughter.

Their mother raised her finger to her lips. "Shhh! Let's eat, and then we'll go back in and see how he's doing."

Rory had become so engrossed in his movie by the

time they came back in that he didn't even seem to realize they'd been gone. Ashleigh noticed his plate was clean, too. She smiled and thought that maybe when he was better, she *would* give him more rides on Moe.

Mona's first question when Ashleigh got on the bus the next morning was, "How was Lightning?"

"I couldn't go."

Mona looked at her in surprise. "Were you afraid to go alone?"

"Well, a little, but that wasn't the reason." Ashleigh explained about Rory's accident and the extra hours she'd had to work in the barn.

"Oh, I'm sorry," Mona sympathized. "I hope Rory's going to be okay."

"He will. I'll go up to see Lightning this afternoon. Do you still want to come?"

"Yes, definitely."

"We'll make it a quick trip," Ashleigh added. "I have to be careful not to do anything dumb, or I won't be able to go to the Derby. You know my parents will keep their word and make me stay home if I break the rules. They could do it, too, because Kurt would be there to keep an eye on me."

"When does he keep an eye on anything?" Mona asked. "I hardly ever see him."

"Last night he slept in the barn so he could make sure Impish was okay. She hasn't foaled yet. Last year her foal nearly died, and would have if Mom and Dad hadn't been there to save it." Ashleigh paused and considered.

"Well, it's sweet that Kurt was worried about her," Mona said.

Ashleigh nodded. "I think Kurt has a secret."

"What do you mean?" Mona asked. "Do you think he's a criminal or something, like Mr. Nasty?"

"No, more like a horse person who had bad luck. Dad sometimes tells me about jockeys and trainers and conditioners who've had bad luck. And the way Kurt always keeps to himself . . . there's something mysterious about it."

"He's too big to have been a jockey," Mona said.

"Yeah, but I wonder if he used to work on a big breeding farm or for a big racing stable, something like that."

"Your parents must have checked before they hired him."

Ashleigh frowned. "Yeah, they would have. Maybe I should ask them."

"Maybe," Mona said. "Anyway, it's supposed to rain

today. Are you going to check on Lightning if it does?"

Ashleigh had noticed the darkening clouds before she got on the bus. Going to Lightning's barn with a heavy load of feed would be tricky enough without a rainstorm. "I'm going to try," she said. "Do you still want to come with me, even if it's raining?"

Mona considered for a second, then nodded. "Yes. If our parents ask why we're riding in the rain, we can tell them we're trying to get ourselves and the ponies used to riding in all kinds of weather. What do you think? Will they believe it?"

Ashleigh considered. "Yes," she said. "They know we're nuts about riding."

"Nuts about *horses!*" Mona added.

It was just starting to drizzle when Ashleigh got Moe out of the paddock that afternoon. She'd ridden in much worse weather, so she wasn't concerned. Still, she decided to wear her foul-weather slicker. Mona arrived on Silver a few minutes later and led him into the barn as Ashleigh finished tacking up Moe.

"Good, you wore your slicker, too," Ashleigh said to her friend.

"It's only drizzling, but I figured I should be prepared."

Ashleigh tightened the girth on Moe's saddle, then went into the empty stall behind her to collect the bundle of hay she'd left there. "Now all I have to do is figure out how to tie this hay to Moe's saddle so it doesn't fall off."

"Want some help?" Mona asked.

"Sure."

The girls worked quickly. Ashleigh's parents were in town running errands, but Kurt was around somewhere. Ashleigh didn't want to risk having him ask why she was carting hay along on a trail ride.

"It's going to be a tight fit," Mona said, "with both you and a load of hay in the saddle."

"I'll manage." Ashleigh tied off the last of the burlap twine around the saddle leathers. "That should do it. Let's go."

As they released the ponies from the crossties, Ashleigh glanced up the barn aisle and saw Kurt standing at the end, staring at them.

Oh, no! she thought. *Did he see the hay?*

Kurt was frowning, but then he turned and left the barn by the side door.

Ashleigh drew in a relieved sigh. He must not have noticed anything strange.

Ashleigh and Mona quickly led Moe and Silver outside, mounted, and urged the ponies forward in the
misty rain. When they were halfway up the hill
behind the paddocks, they kicked the ponies into a
canter over the damp grass.

"Lightning, here we come," Ashleigh called softly.

9

The rain started coming down in sheets about half an hour later, but by that time Ashleigh and Mona were too close to Lightning's farm to turn back. Fortunately Ashleigh's orange ties had held to the branches, because it was almost impossible for the girls to see any other landmarks. They pulled their rain hoods further over their heads and battled on until they were above Lightning's pasture. They stopped the ponies.

As they looked down at the ramshackle farm, the rain gradually eased and became a steady drizzle again. But with every breeze, the trees above their heads released a shower of water droplets. Ashleigh was glad to see that Mr. Nasty hadn't left Lightning out in the rain. She glanced toward the farmhouse. The windows were dark, even in the rainy gloom. Either Mr. Nasty didn't believe in wasting electricity or he wasn't home. She hoped it was the latter.

"I don't see his truck," Mona said.

"No, but maybe he parked it somewhere else. We'd better wait."

The forest was silent except for the drip of water falling from the trees. Then suddenly Ashleigh heard a sound behind them in the woods—the crunch of something heavy on wet leaves. She stiffened and listened more carefully. Was Lightning's owner in the woods somewhere, watching them? She heard another rustling sound.

"Mona, did you hear anything?" she whispered urgently.

"No . . ." But Mona sat stock still as she listened, too.

A moment passed, but all was silent. "I must have been imagining things," Ashleigh murmured. "I'm so nervous."

Luckily the ponies were cooperating and hadn't made any noises of protest at being held standing in the rain. After about ten minutes, there was still no sign of life on the farm.

"Should we risk going down to the barn?" Ashleigh asked.

"Yes, but I think we should go on foot."

Ashleigh nodded. "We can tie the ponies here." They dismounted and secured the ponies' reins.

Ashleigh untied the wrapped bundle of hay from Moe's back. Mona helped her carry it. The girls stayed close to the tree line as they worked their way toward the barn. They would have to risk crossing a few yards of open space if they were going to get into the barn, but they had no choice.

When they were directly across from the barn door, Ashleigh hesitated. She checked the house and the drive.

"Ready?" she whispered to Mona.

Mona nodded.

Taking a deep breath, Ashleigh dashed across the pasture and into the barn, Mona at her heels.

The interior smelled no better than the last time they'd been inside. In fact, because of all the dampness, the odor of dirty bedding was stronger. Lightning was tied in her stall. She turned her head to look at the girls and softly nickered.

Ashleigh and Mona exchanged a happy look. She recognized them—as friends. Ashleigh lowered the bale of hay to the floor and stepped closer to examine Lightning. Her coat was slightly damp, but the moisture hadn't penetrated through the outer layers. Ashleigh wondered if it was her imagination, or if the mare seemed brighter and more alert. Could the feed they left for her have made a difference already? The mare certainly didn't look any less skeletal, but her eyes weren't as dull.

"We have to hurry," Mona whispered.

The girls worked quickly, unwrapping the hay and putting it in the least dirty corner of her stall where she could still reach it. Ashleigh unzipped her backpack and placed several handfuls of feed next to the hay. She wished she could have brought a feed bucket, but they couldn't leave behind any signs that might give away their presence to Mr. Nasty.

"Okay, let's go," Ashleigh murmured. They both hugged Lightning's neck, but they couldn't risk staying longer. Lightning had already dropped her head to the food and was making quick work of eating it as Ashleigh and Mona left the barn and sprinted across the drive.

Neither spoke until they were safely hidden in the woods. "I hope she eats all that before he gets back," Mona said. "I'm so afraid he'll notice that we've been around."

"She was doing a pretty good job of it when we left," Ashleigh said. "But I know what you mean. It scares me, too."

"You've got your backpack?" Mona asked.

Ashleigh allowed herself a grin. "Yup, and the wrapping I put around the hay."

"Just checking," Mona said. "Let's hurry. It looks like it's going to start pouring again."

When they reached the ponies, they mounted quickly and heeled them to a trot up the trail away from the farm. Now that their mission was over, both girls were shivering from the damp, but their trip had been a success.

They'd reached the spring and were on the last leg of their journey home when Ashleigh looked back over her shoulder and felt a chill. "Mona, I keep having this feeling that someone is following us."

Mona glanced at her, puzzled. "I don't get that feeling, Ash. You're probably still spooked about Mr. Nasty finding us."

Ashleigh wasn't sure about that, but she nodded. "I guess."

When they got back to Edgardale, both Ashleigh's parents came out of the barn as if they'd been waiting.

"I'd like to know what you girls think you were up to," Mr. Griffen said crossly. "A short ride in this weather is okay, but you've been gone for over an hour. Mona's mother has called twice. Did you think about your ponies getting drenched and chilled? To say nothing of yourselves! Mona, go use the office phone and call your mother. Ashleigh, get Moe settled and rubbed down. And make sure that pony is dry and blanketed before you start your chores!"

"You know I'd never put Moe away wet, Dad," Ashleigh said, hurt.

Her father seemed too angry to respond. "And make sure Silver gets similar treatment."

Both girls scrambled, Mona running toward the stable office and Ashleigh hurriedly leading both ponies into the barn, where she put them in crossties and began untacking them. She couldn't believe her father was so angry. What had she and Mona done wrong except ride in the rain? And it hadn't been raining that hard when they left.

Mona came down the barn aisle after talking to her mother. Her cheeks were pale, and she was shivering even more than when they'd been drenched on the trail. "My mom's coming to pick me up in half an hour. She was really mad," Mona told her. "Your father said that I can leave Silver here for the night. Ash, I didn't think we'd get in a mess like this."

"Neither did I," Ashleigh said, suddenly feeling guilty. "You wouldn't be in a mess if I hadn't asked you to come today."

"I *wanted* to come," Mona said. "You didn't have to persuade me!"

Mona threw her arms around Ashleigh, and they hugged. Ashleigh felt choked up. "Thanks for being my best friend, Mona."

"You too, Ash."

They went to their ponies and finished untacking them. "The only dry part of this saddle is where I sat," Mona said. "But why are our parents so mad at us? We weren't out that long, and we came home way before you had to start your chores."

"I can tell you why," Kurt said from behind them.

Ashleigh stared at him. If the barn cat had suddenly started speaking to her, she wouldn't have been more surprised. She also noticed that Kurt's hat was soaking wet, as was his hair. He must have been out in the downpour, too, bringing in the Edgardale horses.

"They're still worried after you got lost," he said. "They overreacted."

It was probably the longest speech Ashleigh had ever heard from Kurt's lips unless he was talking about horses.

It took a moment before Ashleigh could speak. "Do you really think so?"

Kurt shrugged. "Parents worry. Let me take that

pony from you," he added to Mona, unclipping Silver's crossties. "Let's get him in a stall, where he'll be more comfortable."

As Kurt led Silver away, Mona turned to Ashleigh with wide, questioning eyes.

Ashleigh shrugged, equally mystified.

"You ought to take Moe into his stall, too," Kurt called over his shoulder to Ashleigh.

They all worked steadily for the next half hour in near silence. Kurt first helped Mona with Silver, then walked across the barn aisle to help Ashleigh with Moe. Both ponies were now fairly dry and buckled into their blankets.

"I'll go mix them up some hot bran mash," Kurt said, and walked away.

Mona motioned Ashleigh over. "What was that all about?"

"I don't know," Ashleigh said. "He's never acted like this. It's kind of weird."

"How could he be so sure what our parents were thinking?" Mona asked.

"Remember I said I thought he had a past?"

"Everyone has a past," Mona said. "Even us, and we're only ten."

"Yeah, but maybe his past has something to do with his coming here to work as a groom and handyman and never saying much. He knows a lot more than that—he knows tons about horses. I think he's got a secret."

"Ashleigh, you're making up things about people again, like they're characters in books or something."

Ashleigh flushed. Then she mentally shook herself. Why should she feel guilty about having a vivid imagination? What was wrong with having fantasies, like her dream of winning the Kentucky Derby on a horse bred by her parents? And maybe Kurt *did* have a mysterious past.

But any comment she was going to make was cut short when Kurt suddenly appeared with the bran mash for each of the ponies.

Mona's mother honked her car horn from the drive.

"I've got to go!" Mona cried. Her mother was a horse lover, but she also had a full-time job at a lawyer's office and was on her way home from work. Mona ran to Silver's stall and gave her pony a goodnight kiss.

"Hope we're not in too much trouble," Ashleigh said, walking her friend to the door. "The Derby's in a week, and I want to go *so* much." Ashleigh was silent for a second. "But I want to save Lightning, too! I hope your mom's not too mad, Mona."

"Me too. See you on the bus in the morning."

Ashleigh prolonged her chores as much as she could. When she finally went up to the house, she found her family just sitting down around the kitchen table. Rory had recovered enough to be able to sit in his own chair.

The conversation around the table was as usual—her parents asking about her and Caro's school day, then talking about farm business. They discussed which mares had been bred to which stallions and what the likely outcome of the match would be.

It wasn't until Caroline was starting to clear the table that Mr. Griffen said to Ashleigh, "I hope we won't have a repeat of today's adventures." He looked at her, and she tried to return his gaze. "No more risking the ponies."

"I promise, Dad."

"I don't know what you were up to today, but your mother reminded me of the mischief we used to get into when we were kids. Innocent high jinks are one thing. Deliberately breaking rules is another."

"Yes, Dad." Ashleigh lowered her eyes, afraid her father would read the truth in them.

"Go up to your room and do your homework. And you'd better be on your best behavior from here on out, or no Derby. Am I making myself clear?"

Ashleigh nodded, then beat a retreat toward the stairs and her room. Caroline came up a few minutes later as Ashleigh was carefully doing her math homework.

"What's this?" Caroline said, giving Ashleigh a surprised look. "No horse magazine covering your notebook?" She glanced over Ashleigh's shoulder. "Hey, and you've even got the answers right. Will miracles never cease?"

"Oh, stuff it, Caro," Ashleigh said, irritated. But she was secretly happy that her sister had done her double checking for her—Caroline was a whiz at math. Now she wouldn't have to go over each of the problems herself. "Maybe I hate math, but I can beat you any day in English."

"Oh, yeah?" Caroline said halfheartedly. She sat down in front of her dressing table. As always, Caroline had already done her own homework. She reached for a bottle of nail polish.

Ashleigh rolled her eyes. "Oh, yuck, Caro. You're not going to put that ugly color on your nails?"

Caroline frowned. "What's wrong with it? Everybody's wearing this color."

"Right," Ashleigh shot back, "if you want to look like you just climbed out of Dracula's coffin."

"What do you know?" Caroline said tersely, but Ashleigh noticed that her sister put the bottle back and reconsidered her choice of colors. Ashleigh smiled to herself. At least one person in the family still trusted her.

10

"What did your mother say?" Ashleigh asked Mona on the bus the next morning. "Was she really mad?"

"Yeah, but Kurt was right. I think she was more worried than anything. She called our house from work, and when I didn't answer, she figured I was at your house. Because of the rain, she wanted me to stay there until she picked me up. She didn't know you and I were out riding until your parents told her, and she was pretty upset when she found out."

"You didn't get grounded or anything, did you?" Ashleigh asked.

"No, but I'd better not get into any more trouble. What about you?" Mona asked.

"My dad was pretty clear," Ashleigh said. "No going to the Derby if I mess up again. But that's not what I'm worried about. What are we going to do about Lightning?"

Mona shook her head. "I don't know," she said sadly. "I hate to see her suffering. But, Ash, I don't dare go up there again. You understand, don't you?" She looked over at her friend with pleading eyes.

Ashleigh nodded. She had thought long and hard about it and knew Mona was right. But her heart ached for the poor mare.

At lunch that day at their usual cafeteria table, Ashleigh and Mona sat with Lynne and Jamie. Lynne was totally excited and nervous about her horse show that weekend. Since it was Friday, she had only twenty-four hours to go.

"You'll be there, right?" she asked the other three girls.

"We'll be there," Mona answered. "I want to learn to jump, so I'm really going to be concentrating on what the riders do."

"I hope you won't be concentrating on me too much," Lynne said. "I'm already so nervous, I can't stand it."

"Don't worry," Jamie said. "You're going to do fine once you're in the show ring. I've seen you jump, and you're good."

"Thanks." Lynne flushed. "But let's talk about

116

something else. Ash, who do you think is going to win the Derby next weekend?"

"An underdog," said Ashleigh. "Woodland Sprite. She's the only filly in the race."

"You think she can win?" Jamie asked. "She's never raced against colts. I'd say she's a real long shot. Or do you have some inside information?" she added with a grin.

Ashleigh laughed. "Nope. I just like her. Who do you like?"

"Tough Love," Jamie said. "I don't see how anyone can beat him. He'll be the favorite. But you're going to see one of your horses race, aren't you?"

"Yup, Wanderer's Quest in the Providian Mile. She's a daughter of our best mare, and I took care of her when she was a baby. She wasn't called Wanderer's Quest then, though. Anyway, her current owners have box seats for the Derby and have invited my family."

"My dad got us tickets through the track where he announces, so maybe I'll see you there," said Jamie. "If we can find each other in the crowd, that is. It's going to be mobbed!"

For nearly a week Ashleigh stayed away from Lightning, but the poor mare was constantly in her thoughts. What was happening up at that ramshackle farm? Was her owner feeding her? Was he working her until she was ready to drop in her tracks? It tore at Ashleigh to have no answers. She tried to keep busy so that she wouldn't have time to think about the situation, but that didn't always work.

On Saturday she and Mona had gone to Lynne's show and had been there to cheer when Lynne and her Welsh pony, Lance, had a clear round over the fences. The fences weren't high, but the course was tricky, and Ashleigh felt proud of Lynne's efforts. Still, as much as she liked to watch the jumpers, Ashleigh knew it wasn't for her. Her dream was to be in the saddle of a powerful Thoroughbred, crouching low over its shoulders with the wind in her face as they roared around a racetrack at unbelievable speeds.

At home, Ashleigh spent double time on her chores and playing with the rapidly growing foals to keep her mind off Lightning. Impish, their last mare to give birth, successfully foaled on Sunday morning. Ashleigh watched with her parents, Rory, and Kurt as the newborn filly struggled to her feet only a half hour after birth.

"She's going to be a strong one," Mr. Griffen said, looking pleased. He put his arm around his wife's shoulders. "Well, Elaine, we sure can't complain about this year's crop. We haven't lost a single foal, and they all look above average to me."

Mrs. Griffen chuckled. "I'd say you and I are just a little bit prejudiced, but you're right. It's been a very good year."

Knock wood, Ashleigh thought. She knew how quickly things could go from good to bad on a breeding farm.

All the Griffens were getting excited about going to the Derby on Saturday, but Ashleigh couldn't get her mind off Lightning. Finally on Friday Ashleigh decided she couldn't stand the worried torment any longer. She had visions of Lightning slowly starving or being worked so hard, she collapsed and died.

Ashleigh didn't tell Mona what she'd decided to do—she'd already gotten her friend into enough trouble.

It was an absolutely beautiful, sunny spring day, perfect for riding. No would give a second thought about her taking Moe out. She just *had* to see if the mare was all right. If something went wrong and she was late getting home, she might lose her chance of going to the Derby. But somehow, the Derby didn't seem so important compared to Lightning.

She finished her homework as soon as she got home from school, did some early chores, then saddled up Moe, put some grain in her backpack, and headed up the now familiar trail to Lightning's farm.

Ashleigh promised herself that she was only going to check on the mare and drop feed along the pasture fence, and then she would be out of there. Yet she was still nervous as she and Moe followed the tape-marked trail to the farm. She was so intent on her mission that she nearly jumped out of her skin when she startled the deer herd near the spring. In her concern about Lightning, she had forgotten all about the deer. She watched as they bounded off through the woods, white tails raised high in alarm. Seeing the beautiful creatures made her feel a little better.

When she reached the end of the trail, Ashleigh kept Moe hidden behind the trees, as usual. But as she peered down into Lightning's pasture she felt the blood drain from her face.

Lightning's owner was standing over the mare, whip in his hand, lashing it over her back and hindquarters.

"You lousy excuse for a horse! Suddenly you get feisty and kick me! I'll show you. You'll work for me or I'll beat you senseless."

The mare made an effort to bolt away from him and his whip, but he held tight to the lead rope attached to her halter. There was nowhere for

Lightning to go as he lashed out with the whip again. She whinnied in pain and distress.

"And why are you so feisty, I'd like to know? Maybe I've been feeding you more than you need, huh?" he muttered.

Ashleigh felt a chill run up her spine. Were she and Mona responsible for the beating Lightning was getting? Was it possible that the extra food had given her the strength to fight back against her cruel owner?

The man lifted his whip again. Ashleigh could see bloody welts appearing through Lightning's shaggy coat.

She wanted to race down to the pasture and stop the man, but she knew she couldn't. He wouldn't listen to her, and he'd already threatened to call the police—or use his gun—if he caught her or Mona on his property again. Besides, if she interfered, he might only beat Lightning worse than he already was.

By now, Lightning's head was down. There was no fire left in her soul. The man had her where he wanted her—broken and submissive.

He tucked his whip under his arm and started leading Lightning out of the pasture. She went quietly, with no will left to protest. Ashleigh felt helpless and devastated. She'd never dreamed that by trying to help Lightning, she would make things worse for the poor horse!

Ashleigh spun Moe around and kicked him into as fast a trot as the narrow path would allow. Tears flooded her eyes and rolled down her cheeks as they rushed up the trail. She was so worried, she was barely conscious of where she was going.

I have to do something, she thought frantically. *I have to tell Mom and Dad. I don't care what they do to me!*

She couldn't let things go on the way they were. That horrible man might even kill Lightning!

They'll be mad at me, she thought as she crossed the pastures of Edgardale. *Even madder than usual, because I lied to them for so long.*

But she had no choice.

Feeling numb, Ashleigh brought Moe into the barn, untacked him, and led him into his stall. She was still crying; she couldn't seem to stop. Her despair was so great that even Moe sensed it and touched his velvet nose to her cheek as if to comfort her.

"Thanks, boy," she whispered, stroking his head. "I know you want to help, but I've got to do this by myself."

She left Moe's stall and saw Kurt approaching with water buckets in hand. Ashleigh knew that there was no way he could miss seeing her tears, and he didn't. He stopped a few feet away from her and put down his buckets.

"Something wrong with Moe?" he asked with a touch of alarm.

Ashleigh shook her head, not daring to speak.

Kurt frowned. "Then what is it? Anything I can do to help?"

Avoiding his gaze, Ashleigh shook her head more firmly. She quickly picked up Moe's tack and headed down the aisle to the tack room. She didn't want to be rude, but she knew she'd break down in another bout of sobs if she lingered any longer. She could tell that Kurt was still watching her, but she didn't turn around. Instead, she rushed to the tack room and stayed there, carefully stowing away Moe's saddle, bridle, and saddle pad. When she looked back out into the barn, there was no sign of Kurt. Ashleigh jogged down the aisle and outside. She knew she had to act quickly, or she wouldn't act at all.

Her mother was in the kitchen, preparing dinner before going back out to bring in the horses for the night. Fortunately, Caroline and Rory weren't around. Ashleigh saw her mother's welcoming smile but felt too guilty to return it. She squared her shoulders.

"Mom, I have to talk to you and Dad."

Her mother's hand paused over the vegetables she was cutting, and her brow wrinkled in concern.

"I can see from your face that this is serious," she said. "You're failing math?"

Ashleigh shook her head. "No, this is much worse."

"Worse?" Mrs. Griffen repeated. "It can't wait, I gather."

"No," Ashleigh said.

Mrs. Griffen put down her knife, wiped her hands on a towel, and walked over to Ashleigh. "Your father's in the den trying to figure out the new computer system. I can't guarantee he'll be in a very good mood, but let's go see him."

She put a hand on Ashleigh's shoulder, and together they walked to the den. The door was open. Ashleigh saw her father hunched over the keyboard. The desk was cluttered with instruction manuals. He made a growling noise in his throat as something flashed up on the screen.

"No!" he muttered. "That's not what you were supposed to do!"

Ashleigh's mother called quietly from the doorway. "Derek, do you have a minute?"

He started, then turned, running his fingers through his thick hair. "I hate these machines. I'd rather work on my old account books." He paused when he saw Ashleigh's tearstained face.

"Ashleigh wants to talk to us," Mrs. Griffen said.

Mr. Griffen looked at his daughter. "What's up, honey?"

"I've done something pretty bad." Ashleigh swallowed, trying to keep her voice steady. "That day when Mona and me got lost . . . well, we didn't tell you the whole truth. Mona's not so much to blame as me," she quickly added, not wanting to get Mona in trouble.

"Slow down and tell us what happened," Mrs. Griffen instructed her.

Ashleigh took a deep breath. "We did get lost, just like we said, but before we found our way to a road, we came to this deserted farm—only it turned out not to be deserted. We were so lost. We were only trying to find a way out to a road, and there was this overgrown drive in front of the house. But when we rode around the barn trying to get there, we found a horse tied in a stall."

Ashleigh's voice broke as she thought of Lightning, with her sweet, sad eyes. "She was such a mess—half starved and tied in this stall that hadn't been cleaned in a month. We felt so sorry for her." Ashleigh wiped a tear from her cheek, then said in a rush, "I tried to steal her. I mean, not really. But I was letting her loose—I just wanted to get her out of that filthy stall. Then this man came up behind us—"

"Whoa," her father said. "Just slow down a minute. You were letting a horse loose?" he asked in disbelief. "A horse that doesn't belong to us? You can't be serious, Ashleigh."

Ashleigh shuddered. "I *am* serious, Dad. I didn't think of it as stealing—I just wanted to help the horse. But the owner thought it was stealing. He said he was going to call the police and report us. Mona and I were so scared . . . especially when he pointed his shotgun at us."

"He pointed a shotgun at you?" Mrs. Griffen cried in alarm.

"He said he wouldn't put up with trespassers on his property, especially thieving ones." Ashleigh's eyes were welling with guilty tears again.

"But you're a couple of kids!" Mrs. Griffen protested. "I can't believe he pulled a shotgun on children!"

"He didn't use it," Ashleigh said quickly, "at least not until we were back on the ponies. Then he fired it into the air."

Ashleigh realized that both her parents were staring at her in wide-eyed horror. She buried her face in her hands. "I'm sorry . . . I'm so sorry. I didn't mean to get into so much trouble. I just wasn't thinking. . . . Poor Lightning." Her voice broke on a sob.

Then suddenly she felt her mother's arm around her shoulders and heard her father demanding, "Who is this nut who'd fire on a couple of kids? Could you recognize him again, Ashleigh?"

Ashleigh nodded. "But there's more I have to tell you. We went back when he wasn't around so we could try to help the mare and bring her food. One time when we went, he was hooking her up to a harness so she could lift an engine block into the back of his truck. He didn't see us, but he used her so hard, she practically went to her knees, and he didn't feed her afterward."

Ashleigh closed her eyes, remembering.

"We haven't gone up for a week because we almost got caught. That was the day we rode in the rain, and you got so mad. I went up today." Ashleigh opened her eyes and looked up at her mother. "I just had to see if she was all right."

"And was she?" her father asked.

"No," Ashleigh cried. "When I got there, he was beating her with a whip in the pasture, blaming her for being more feisty than usual, and I knew she was more feisty because we had been bringing her extra feed."

Her parents were silent for a moment, and each second seemed like an hour to Ashleigh.

"Why didn't you tell us about the horse the day you got lost?" Mrs. Griffen finally asked.

"We were afraid to. The man was going to call the police! I didn't want you to know what I'd done."

"Didn't you and Mona stop to think that we might have been able to help?" Mrs. Griffen continued.

Ashleigh shook her head. "All we could think about was that I'd tried to steal the horse, and Mona was there, too. The police could have arrested us. We didn't know if the man had called them or not. We didn't dare say anything."

"You thought you could save this horse by yourselves?" her father asked.

"I called the humane society, but they knew I was a kid. The woman said she couldn't help unless one of you guys called her. I don't think she believed me." Ashleigh shrugged hopelessly. "I didn't know what else to do."

There was another long silence. Then Ashleigh's mother spoke quietly. "There are a couple of issues here. One, that you tried to steal a horse for humanitarian and caring reasons. The second is that you didn't trust us, your parents, enough to confide in us and ask for our help. That bothers me the most,

Ashleigh. Did you think that we of all people would ignore this poor horse? If you'd confided in us, we could have tried to do something to help long before now."

"We were just so scared, Mom," Ashleigh cried, leaning her head into her mother's shoulder. "We didn't know what to do. We thought you and Mona's parents would be so angry at us—"

"Where exactly is this farm, Ashleigh?" her father asked. "You obviously know how to get there."

Ashleigh nodded. "We followed deer trails from the spring in our woods. That's how we found it. The trails went up over the hill, then down again, then split into a bunch of different trails. That's why we couldn't find our way home the first time. So we just kept following the trail downhill, then found the farm. The farm's drive comes out on the road to Meyersville. There's no mailbox or anything, and the driveway goes through the woods for a long time."

Her father glanced at his watch. "The humane society should still be open. Let me give them a call. And I think I'll call the police, too."

Ashleigh felt as though all the breath had been sucked out of her. "The police? Please, Dad, no! I promise I'll never do anything bad ever again—ever!"

Her father looked at her stricken face and almost

smiled. "Ash, I'm not calling the police to report *you*. I'm calling to report the horse and the madman who dared to shoot his gun at you and Mona. Describe the mare's condition to me again."

"Skinny, every bone showing through her coat, about fifteen or sixteen hands, nice conformation, but she barely had the strength to lift her head. When I saw her this afternoon, he'd beaten her with a whip, and she had bloody welts showing."

Her father got on the phone. Ashleigh listened to his one-sided conversation with someone at the local humane society, who at least seemed to take *him* seriously. Before he called the police, Mrs. Griffen led her out of the room. "It's time to bring in the horses. Come and help me. Your father will do everything he can."

Ashleigh followed her mother, stunned by her conversation with her parents. She'd been so sure that they would be furious and would ground her for a month. She felt almost dizzy with astonishment at their understanding and support.

Yet a few minutes later, as she and her mother started leading the mares and foals into the barn for the night, she had an even more astounding surprise when she looked up to see Kurt leading a horse down the lane between the paddocks from the general direction of the woods.

Ashleigh stopped and stared in the growing twilight. She blinked and stared again. Yes, the horse was white. She blinked again. Yes, the horse was shaggy-coated; it was skin and bones.

It was Lightning!

Ashleigh let out a yelp. "Mom, it's her!"

Then she sprinted off toward Kurt and Lightning, meeting up with them just as they reached the end of the grassy lane. With a huge grin, she flung her arms around Lightning's shaggy neck. As if she sensed she was finally safe, the mare nickered in response.

"Oh, Lightning, you're here! I can hardly believe it!" Ashleigh glanced up at Kurt. "But how did you know? How did you find her?"

"I followed you and your friend one day when you went up there to feed her. I noticed you bundling up some hay and didn't think you were taking it for your ponies."

Ashleigh gasped. "I had a feeling someone was following us!"

"Sorry if I frightened you, but I wondered what

you girls were up to. I wanted to make sure you were okay."

"Ashleigh," Mrs. Griffen called, walking briskly toward them, "what's going on? Who's this horse?" Then she stopped and looked carefully at the mare. "It's not—"

"It is, Mom," Ashleigh cut in. "It's Lightning, the mare we were trying to save."

"But I don't understand," she said, frowning at Kurt. "What are you doing with the mare? Is this Ashleigh's doing?"

He quickly cut in. "My bringing the mare here has nothing to do with Ashleigh. I acted on my own." He explained how he'd followed the girls and had admired how they were trying to help. Then this afternoon he'd seen Ashleigh come home in tears.

"She'd just untacked Moe," he said, "so I knew she'd come back from a ride. But when I saw her tears— and you have to do a lot of crying to have such swollen, red eyes—I guessed where she'd been and went up to check."

"You just went up and *took* the mare?" Mrs. Griffen gasped. "But, Kurt, that's horse theft!"

"I called the police first and told them what I was doing and where I was taking the mare. The sheriff's office said they would check it out, although I couldn't give them any directions to the farm except from here on foot or horseback."

Ashleigh saw her father walking toward them. "I just got off the phone from the sheriff's office, Ashleigh. They're sending someone over. They've already had a report on this horse from one of our employees."

He looked from Kurt to Ashleigh. "What's going on here? That's the horse, I gather," he added, walking over to Lightning. He quickly inspected her and cursed under his breath. "Poor thing. She's a mess, all right."

"Yes," Mrs. Griffen agreed. "It takes a lot of neglect before any horse looks this bad."

Kurt and Ashleigh repeated their stories. By then, a patrol car was pulling down the drive. They all turned as an officer got out and approached them. "Are you Derek Griffen?" he asked Ashleigh's father.

"Yes, I called about an abused horse."

The officer looked toward Lightning. "Is this the horse in question?"

"Yes," Derek Griffen said.

"We received another call about this horse earlier from one of your employees. . . ." He checked his notes. "Kurt Bradley."

"That was me," Kurt replied.

The officer nodded and walked over to inspect Lightning. A moment later he turned away in disgust. "No one has the right to treat an animal this way. We have an officer out looking for the property. It's hard to find. Can anyone give me more information?"

Ashleigh spoke up quickly. "The driveway's off the Meyersville road, on the right side coming from here. It's not marked, but it's near the gates of Stoneycrop Farm, on the other side of the street." Ashleigh tried to describe whatever landmarks she'd seen before it had gotten dark.

The officer nodded to her. "Your father said that you were lost when you came across the mare."

"Yes. We'd been following some deer trails in the woods."

Mr. Griffen interrupted. "I did tell your dispatcher that this madman shot at the girls?"

The officer nodded. "Let me contact the other officer with these directions. Then we can decide what should be done with the horse."

"She can stay here," Ashleigh said quickly, giving her parents a pleading look. "We have extra stalls."

Mr. Griffen nodded. "For tonight, at any rate. I don't know what the laws are concerning abused animals. We'll have to see what the humane society people say."

The officer strode back to his car.

"They won't send her back to him?" Ashleigh cried.

"No, I'm certain they won't do that," her father replied. "Your mom and I will fight tooth and nail to see that they don't. Why don't you and Kurt take the mare inside, clean her up and treat those welts, and give her hay and water? We'll call you if the officer has any more questions for you."

Ashleigh nodded, then followed Kurt and Lightning off to the barn.

"I'm so happy that you went and got her," Ashleigh told Kurt. "I've been afraid to tell my parents about her."

"Why?" Kurt asked.

Ashleigh explained to him what she and Mona had been doing when they got caught. "But after I saw what he did to her today, I knew I had to tell them and ask them to help."

Kurt was silent for a moment. "I'll bet they weren't as angry as you thought they'd be."

Ashleigh looked at him in surprise. "No, they weren't. They were more upset that Lightning's owner had shot at us. How did you know?"

He sighed heavily. When he spoke, his voice was so soft that Ashleigh had trouble hearing him. "I had a daughter your age. She died last year of leukemia."

Ashleigh's eyes brimmed with tears. "How awful. I'm so sorry."

"It was the most painful moment in my life and always will be. That's why I came to work here—I had to get away from anything that reminded me of her. Her mother and I were divorced, so I sold my breeding farm in New York state and came down here." He paused.

It was the most Ashleigh had ever heard him say, and now she could understand why. "But you know, meeting you and your friend has helped me," he added. "You girls did something I'd have been proud of my daughter doing . . . if she'd lived."

Ashleigh didn't know what to say, but Kurt didn't seem to expect any response. "Well, let's get to work on this little lady. She sure needs our help."

They installed Lightning in a big box stall, and while Ashleigh got the mare hay and water, Kurt collected supplies to clean and dress her wounds. As Lightning munched the hay, Ashleigh and Kurt worked together in near silence, bathing the mare with warm water, drying her, cleaning her wounds, and applying antiseptic ointment. Ashleigh gently brushed Lightning's shaggy coat, freeing bunches of winter hair she'd yet to shed. Next she attacked the tangles in the mare's long mane and tail, finally resorting to cutting out the worst ones.

Kurt examined and worked on the mare's feet, filing and cutting off excess growth, much the way Ashleigh would clip her own fingernails. He carefully checked her teeth, which would need filing, too, although they'd bring in a professional to do that.

Already Lightning was looking better, though it would take weeks before she gained enough weight to fill out the hollows between her ribs.

Ashleigh was concentrating so hard that she barely even noticed when her parents appeared at the stall door.

"You'll be glad to hear, Ash," Mr. Griffen said, "that the officer's supervisor agreed the horse could stay here. I have a feeling he didn't have a clue what to do with her, anyway, and was happy that we'd offered to keep her for a while. The officer will be back in touch with us when he has more information."

He opened the stall door and stepped inside. "Let's have a good look at her. Did you find anything serious, Kurt?"

"Nothing obvious. A vet should take a look at her, though. She'll probably need worming, and her teeth need filing. Otherwise, she seems to be in fairly good shape, considering."

"A tough lady, are you?" Mr. Griffen said as he examined the mare. "She's tall. I wonder what her breeding is—she might have some Thoroughbred blood. I'd love to know how she got into that monster's hands. She doesn't look that old, either. I'd say twelve at the max."

Kurt nodded. "I thought I'd give her a little grain."

"Not too much, though, after the way she's been half starved. Some time in the pasture should work wonders, too." He turned to leave the stall, but before he did he ruffled Ashleigh's hair and smiled. "Feeling better now?"

"Oh, yes, Dad! I'm so glad she's here!"

"In that case, I don't suppose you'd mind being responsible for her care."

"Of course not!" Ashleigh said, then chuckled. She realized her father was teasing her. He knew she'd spend every spare moment with Lightning.

"Well, we still have more horses to bring in. Kurt, can you give Elaine and me a hand?"

"Sure."

When the adults left, Ashleigh leaned her cheek against Lightning's freshly groomed neck. "Oh, girl, I'm so, so happy! You're safe now. That nasty man's never going to touch you again. You're going to get lots of love and care, and you'll never go hungry again. You'll be my special horse. Everything's going to be wonderful."

As if responding to the love in Ashleigh's voice, Lightning turned her head and touched her nose to Ashleigh's shoulder.

When Ashleigh woke the next morning, she knew it was a special day. It was Derby day! But more important, Lightning was in a stall in their barn, safe and sound. Ashleigh jumped out of bed, pulled on jeans and a sweatshirt, and hurried out to Lightning's stall. Ashleigh grinned from ear to ear when she heard the mare's welcoming nicker. She let herself into the stall and went to Lightning's side.

"Good morning, girl," she said, hugging the mare's neck. "It's a beautiful one, too. I'm going to put you out in the paddock with Moe today. You remember Moe, my pony. There's tons of thick grass out there, and you can graze to your heart's content!"

As Ashleigh headed to the feed room, her mother walked out of the stable office. "All ready for Churchill Downs?" she asked with a smile. "We have to leave by eight, so we're going to have to do the chores in half the time this morning."

"Eight?" Ashleigh cried. Somehow she hadn't thought they'd be leaving that early. That meant she'd have hardly any time to spend with Lightning, and they wouldn't be back until after dark. Suddenly going to the Derby didn't seem quite so enticing.

"Is something wrong, Ashleigh?" her mother asked.

Ashleigh glanced at her mom. "Well, it's just that with Lightning here now . . ."

"You don't want to leave her."

Ashleigh nodded. "Would you be angry if I didn't go to the Derby?"

"But I thought you were excited about going."

"I am . . . I mean, I was. But that was before Lightning. I'd feel bad leaving her alone on her first day here. She might think I was deserting her."

Her mother considered. "Ashleigh, I know your father put you in charge of her care, but do you think it's smart to bond too closely with the mare, especially since we don't know if she's going to stay here permanently?"

Ashleigh knew her mother was right, but she couldn't bear to spend the whole day away from Lightning when the mare had been on the farm for only one night. What if the humane society people came and took her away while they were gone?

"I'll talk to your father," Mrs. Griffen said.

Ashleigh spent the next hour hurrying through her chores. Caroline and Rory were at work, too. "I don't know why you'd want to stay here when you could be doing something really fun," Caroline said. "You can hang around with the horses here anytime, but you sure can't go to the Derby every day. Do you know how many famous people are going to be there? Movie and TV stars."

"And famous horses, too," Rory put in.

"And you'd rather stay here to look after a bony mare," Caroline added. "You're losing it, Ashleigh."

Ashleigh knew Caroline would never understand her desire to be with Lightning, but Caro's comments reminded her, too, how special the Derby was and how much she'd miss if she stayed home. Ashleigh thought about her sister's words as she finished her chores. She saw Kurt coming down the aisle. He stopped outside the stall Ashleigh was cleaning.

"Lightning is looking much better this morning," he said.

Ashleigh smiled and nodded. "Thanks for helping me so much, Kurt!"

"No problem. I guess you're looking forward to going to the Derby. Pretty exciting day."

Ashleigh's smile faltered. "Well, actually, I was thinking of not going. I don't want to leave Lightning on her first day here."

"I understand," Kurt said thoughtfully. "But you

142

know, you can't go to the Kentucky Derby and have clubhouse seats every day of the year. It's an opportunity most people never have. And I'll be here to look after the mare."

"But I feel like I'd be neglecting her."

"After all she's been through, she's not going to be upset with you for not spending every minute of the day with her. She's out in a pasture, eating more grass than she's seen in years. She'll be coming in to a big box stall filled with fresh bedding. She'll have a full hay net and water bucket. That poor horse must already feel like she's arrived in paradise."

"But what if someone comes to take her away?" Ashleigh asked worriedly.

"I'll guard her with my life," Kurt said seriously. "No one will take that mare off this farm today or any other day until she's healthy again."

"You promise?"

Kurt smiled and laid a hand over his heart. "I promise. Go to the Derby. Have a good time. She'll be safe."

Ashleigh smiled back at Kurt. "Okay, I'll go. I really do want to see Wanderer's daughter run, and there's a filly running in the Derby that I want to bet on."

Kurt laughed. Ashleigh had never heard him laugh before—it was a beautiful, joyful sound. "Then go to it," he said. "I'll finish your chores. Go get ready."

Giving Kurt another smile, Ashleigh headed to the house to change into the only dressy outfit she owned, a flowered cotton dress that Caroline had picked out for her during the family's last shopping expedition. Before they left the bedroom, Caroline walked over with a wide-brimmed straw hat banded with ribbon and settled it on Ashleigh's head.

"Wear that," Caroline ordered. "You can't go to the Derby without a hat."

"And the field for the Providian is approaching the far turn," called the track announcer at Churchill Downs. Ashleigh leaned forward in her clubhouse box seat. "Come on, Quest, make us proud!" she whispered.

"Mistrex in the lead, Our Tess just outside, then Lidlocker a half length farther back," the announcer cried. "A real battle for the lead between Mistrex and Our Tess. And down the stretch they come! It looks to be a duel to the finish. . . . But wait! Here comes Wanderer's Quest roaring up from the back of the field. This lady is flying! They're at the eighth pole. The leaders are still fighting it out, but Wanderer's Quest is rapidly eating into their lead. Can she do it? Our Tess is dropping back now. Wanderer's Quest is still gaining."

Ashleigh and everyone else in the box screamed their encouragement.

"Here's the wire! A close one, but Wanderer's Quest comes up a neck short. In the Providian, it's Mistrex by a neck, Wanderer's Quest second, and, another length back, Our Tess holding on for third."

Ashleigh groaned with disappointment but watched Wanderer's Quest, a classy black mare who would make her mother proud, power past the winner only a few feet beyond the wire. If the race had been a sixteenth of a mile longer, Quest would have won it.

Neither the mare's owners nor her breeders were entirely disappointed with the finish. "She can only get better from here," Mr. Fontaine said proudly. "Don't you think, Derek?"

"I do indeed," Ashleigh's father responded with a grin. "Nice effort. Very nice effort."

Ashleigh stuck with the filly in the Derby, although the odds were long on Woodland Sprite. She gave her mother six dollars of her hard-earned allowance money to place two-dollar win, place, and show bets on the filly. Her mother looked at the odds board, then back to her daughter. "Playing the long shot today, Ash?" Then she smiled. "Actually, maybe I'll join you. We ladies have to stick together."

"Then I'll bet on her, too," Caroline said, overhearing. "But I still want to bet on the favorite, Tough Love."

Mrs. Griffen nodded and went off to the betting window.

Ashleigh glued her eyes to Woodland Sprite during the post parade. She was a big chestnut filly with elegant lines, but some of the colts she was running against were even bigger. Ashleigh crossed her fingers and wished the filly good luck.

By the time the race began, the final odds on Woodland Sprite were thirty to one. Ashleigh didn't feel too hopeful, especially when the filly remained in the middle of the pack all the way down the backstretch, with the favorite, Tough Love, in second and pressing the pace. The first half went in forty-five seconds—very fast, Ashleigh knew—but the favorite was known to be a speedball who also had the stamina to go the Derby distance of a mile and a quarter.

Then suddenly she saw the filly start edging up. Ashleigh leaned forward in her seat and trained her binoculars on the pack. The announcer was so caught up in the four-horse battle at the front that he didn't seem to notice the filly's move up along the inside rail. The ground along the rail had proved heavy and dead throughout the day, so the other jockeys were avoiding it, leaving a path open for the filly.

Woodland Sprite's jockey took full advantage as the

field started down the stretch toward the wire. The filly started moving up effortlessly. Ashleigh was so shocked, she was speechless.

Suddenly the announcer picked up on the filly's run. "On the inside, skimming the rail," he shouted into his microphone, "is the filly, Woodland Sprite. A shocker. She's up into third. They haven't even seen her coming! Tough Love has a short lead, and as they head for the wire, he's starting to pull away from the competition.

"But here comes the filly! She's up into second, still two lengths short of an upset, but not giving ground, either. And as they hit the wire, it's Tough Love by a length and a half, Woodland Sprite, then Mr. Clean, Reactionary . . ."

Ashleigh turned to her mother and sister in amazement. They all held winning place tickets, and none of them could believe it. They leaned together for a celebratory hug. "I want to own a filly like that someday," Ashleigh said breathlessly. "Only my filly will *win* the Derby."

Caroline laughed. "Right, Ash. Keep dreaming."

An hour later they were on their way home after having dinner with the Fontaines. As the adults talked business Ashleigh's thoughts had turned to Lightning. She knew Kurt would have kept a careful eye on the mare. But how was Lightning adjusting to her first day at Edgardale?

Ashleigh fell asleep during the drive home. She awakened with a jolt when the car stopped in the Edgardale drive and Caroline nudged her in the side. "We're home."

Groggily Ashleigh climbed from the car. She made a beeline for the barn and Lightning's stall. The mare was inside dozing, but at the sound of Ashleigh's footsteps she woke and bared her teeth in a soft whinny that almost looked like a smile.

"I'm glad to see you, too," Ashleigh said, beaming, letting herself into the stall.

She wrapped her arms around Lightning's neck and sighed happily. "I missed you today, but we're going to have fun tomorrow . . . and for a lot of tomorrows."

In answer, Lightning gave a soft sigh of contentment. She had come home.

THOROUGHBRED
Ashleigh

Will Ashleigh lose the horse she loves?

When Ashleigh Griffen first found Lightning, the poor mare was thin and sick. But now, because of Ashleigh's loving care Lightning is a beautiful, healthy horse. Ashleigh dreams of all the wonderful things they will do once her family has officially adopted the mare.

But then the humane society announces that they've found another home for Lightning—and they're going to take her away right before Christmas! Ashleigh is frantic. How can she make them understand that Lightning belongs to *her*?

Read Ashleigh #2: *A Horse for Christmas*

Coming soon from HarperHorizon

THOROUGHBRED

**Don't miss the exciting adventures of
a new generation of Thoroughbred horses
and riders at Whitebrook farm.**

Here's a preview of Thoroughbred #31:
A Home for Melanie

Coming soon from HarperHorizon

"Go, Faith, go," twelve-year-old Melanie Graham cheered as she watched the three-year-old filly race around the training track. Leap of Faith stretched out, her pounding hooves digging into the soft dirt. Leaning low over Pirate Treasure's black mane, Melanie pretended she was the jockey and they were the ones galloping around the oval track.

Sensing her excitement, Pirate danced in place. "Easy, buddy." Melanie relaxed back in the saddle. "You know your racing days are over."

Pirate was blind. Before contracting the disease that had caused his blindness, Pirate had been one of the fastest horses at Whitebrook Farm, a Thoroughbred breeding and training facility in Lexington, Kentucky, that was owned by Ashleigh Griffen and Mike Reese, Melanie's aunt and uncle.

When the farm's vet had first diagnosed Pirate's

problem, the handsome Thoroughbred had been turned out to pasture. He'd become depressed and listless, perking up only when Melanie walked him over to the track to be with the other horses.

Ian McLean, the head trainer at Whitebrook, had allowed Melanie and Pirate to pony racehorses. Now in the mornings, the two of them accompanied the young Thoroughbreds to and from the track and starting gate. It wasn't the same as racing, but Pirate enjoyed being back on the track and had regained some of his appetite and energy.

When Faith flew across the finish line, Melanie shouted, "Yes!" then steered Pirate over to the gap in the railing. Since Pirate couldn't see, he had to trust Melanie completely. Sometimes he would get nervous, especially if there were unfamiliar smells or sounds. But when Melanie used him to pony a horse, he always seemed to know that it was time to settle down.

"Great workout!" Melanie called to Naomi Traeger, Faith's sixteen-year-old exercise rider.

Grinning, Naomi pulled down her dirt-splattered goggles and let them drop around her neck. "She ran like the wind!"

Still excited by her gallop, the chestnut filly jogged through the gap in the fence. Naomi steered Faith next to Pirate, who stood quietly even when the filly bumped into his side. Reaching down, Melanie snapped the lead line onto Faith's bit.

"She's full of herself," Melanie said.

"That's for sure." Naomi let her reins go slack. "I'm glad I have you and Pirate to get me back to the barn."

"Are you through for the morning?"

Naomi nodded. Yesterday it had rained, and she was covered with mud from head to toe. Unsnapping her helmet, she let the strap dangle. Naomi was small, with a muscular build. A long dark braid hung down her back. She was a natural athlete, and Melanie loved watching her ride.

When they reached the training barn Melanie held on to Faith while Naomi dismounted. Whitebrook had three barns arranged in a horseshoe, and this morning the grassy area in the middle bustled with activity. Mares and foals were being led into the main barn to spend the hot day out of the sun, and the two- and three-year-olds in training were being cooled down and hosed off before getting their breakfasts.

When Naomi led Faith away, Melanie dismounted, too. She'd ponied four horses that morning, and though it wasn't as tiring as a riding lesson, she'd been in the saddle since six in the morning. Now it was almost nine, and the summer sun was getting hot.

"I bet you're ready for a brushing and some hay, too," Melanie said to Pirate. The big horse rubbed his forehead against her shoulder. The flies had been bad, and his eyes were tearing.

"We'd better clean out your eyes and put some medicine in them," she added. Pulling the reins over his head, she led him into the training barn. The barn was dark, and fans whirled overhead, so it was as cool as a cave.

After untacking Pirate, she put on his halter and hooked him to crossties in the middle of the aisle. Only then did she pull off her helmet. Her cropped blond hair was plastered to her head with sweat. She ran her fingers through the short mop, knowing there wasn't much she could do to make it look better.

Since he'd only walked and trotted, Pirate wasn't too hot, and a good rubbing with a towel followed by a brushing removed the marks left by his saddle. Melanie picked out his feet, then got his medicine from the supply room.

Pirate was like a big puppy dog—until she tried to put the ointment in his eyes. Then he would raise his head as high as he could, making sure there was no way she could reach him.

"This time I'm not giving up," she warned as she carried over an empty bucket.

She set it in front of him, turned it over, and climbed on top. "Now hold still, silly." She tried to squirt some ointment in his eyes, but he shook his head as if to say, *No way.*

Ten minutes later she'd succeeded in getting a little of the sticky medicine in one eye—and a lot all over her fingers. With a sigh, Melanie dropped her arms. As soon as Pirate realized she'd given up, he lowered his head, nuzzling her in the stomach as if to apologize.

"You didn't win yet." Reaching around to the back pocket of her jeans, she pulled out a chunk of carrot and held it under his nose. When he smelled it, his ears pricked forward. He lipped it from her hand, and while he was crunching, she quickly squeezed ointment in the other eye.

"There!" Melanie smiled triumphantly. The thud of hooves on the aisle floor made her look over her shoulder.

"You're going to spoil that horse," Naomi said. She was walking Faith around the barn to cool her off.

"He already is spoiled," Melanie replied as she

jumped off the bucket. Pirate must have heard or smelled Faith, because he gave a low nicker of greeting. Raising her head, the filly nickered back.

"How was her time?" Melanie asked.

"Great. Tomorrow we're going to have a practice race with two of the other three-year-olds. I hope you and Pirate can pony us. Every time you two have accompanied us to the gate, we've done great. You're our lucky charm."

"Sounds good to me." Melanie grinned as Naomi led Faith in the other direction. Lately she *had* been feeling lucky. Not only was she enjoying Pirate, but she'd had a great visit this weekend with her dad and his girlfriend, Susan. Then she and her cousin, Christina Reese, had gone to a super party.

It's about time things went my way, Melanie thought. Since spring, her life had been full of ups and downs. The ups had been great. But she wanted to forget the downs.

"Melanie! Are you going to Mona's with me?" a voice hollered from the far end of the training barn. It was Christina.

"No!" Melanie shouted back. "I'll see you afterward."

Several times a week Christina rode her Thoroughbred mare, Sterling Dream, to Gardener Farm for lessons with Mona Gardener. Christina was really excited about combined training, a sport also known as eventing.

In combined training, the horse and rider competed in three "tests"—dressage, cross-country jumping, and show jumping. Earlier in the summer Christina and Melanie had attended a riding camp to improve their eventing skills.

Christina had come back from camp and entered a local event at a nearby farm. In contrast, Melanie never wanted to ride another sitting trot or half halt. Ponying racehorses on Pirate had been the perfect break for her.

"Then how about a trail ride with me?" Kevin McLean, Ian McLean's twelve-year-old son, asked. Startled, Melanie turned to see where he was. She spotted him halfway down the aisle, leaning over the bottom half of a stall door. His baseball cap was turned backward and his auburn hair poked from beneath it.

"Have you been in that stall the whole time?" Melanie asked.

He nodded. "Yeah. You and Pirate have some interesting conversations. Though I did notice you do all the talking."

"Oh, shut up." Picking up a plastic currycomb,

Melanie wound up and pitched. It flew through the open top door. Kevin ducked at the last minute, and it missed him by an inch.

Snorting nervously, Pirate pulled back on the crossties. "Whoa." Melanie laid her hand on his neck. "I'm sorry. I forget how skittish you can be."

He rolled his eyes, pawed the floor, then gradually relaxed. Melanie mentally kicked herself. She knew not to roughhouse around the horses, especially the Thoroughbreds. They were too big, high-strung, and unpredictable.

Unsnapping Pirate from the crossties, she led him by his halter to his stall. A flake of hay was waiting in the back corner. Melanie let go of the halter, watching as Pirate ambled inside. Swinging his head from side to side, he used his sense of smell to search for the hay. When he found it, he grabbed a big hunk and chewed greedily.

"So how about a ride before it gets too hot?" Kevin said in Melanie's ear. She whirled in surprise.

"Don't sneak up on me like that!" Melanie gave him an annoyed look. But she wasn't really mad.

"I sneaked up on you because I didn't want to be clobbered with a currycomb again," Kevin said, giving her a lopsided grin.

Melanie smiled back. "Sure, I'd love a trail ride. Trib

needs some exercise. He's getting a huge belly."

"Okay, meet you in the main barn in fifteen minutes."

Melanie watched him leave, then put away her tack and grooming bucket. As she strode across the grassy area to the barn housing the mares and foals, she spotted her aunt and uncle talking to George Ballard, the manager of the stallion barn. Her aunt was frowning. Running a farm like Whitebrook was a lot of work, and one thing Melanie had learned about Ashleigh and Mike was that they were fanatics about the care and training of their horses. It had paid off, too. Whitebrook was known all over the country for its fine Thoroughbreds.

When Ashleigh saw Melanie, her frown changed to a smile, and she waved. Melanie waved back, and her uncle gave her a thumbs-up sign. "Good job this morning!" he called.

"Thanks!" Melanie called back with a grin. The other thing she'd learned about Ashleigh and Mike was that they were a great aunt and uncle. Since she'd arrived, they'd treated her with respect and kindness.

And even though she and Christina had gotten off to a rough start, they'd become close, too. In fact, Melanie realized, it hadn't take long for her to think of Whitebrook as her home.

Kevin was already leading his horse, Jasper, from the barn. "Did you brush him?" Melanie asked as she patted the Anglo-Arab's neck.

"Naw. He's clean."

"You're going to ride in cutoffs?"

"I'm tough. Besides, I'm going bareback." Kevin walked around to Jasper's left side. Springing up, he whipped his right leg over Jasper's rear and landed softly on his back.

Melanie hurried into the tack room to get Trib's bridle. When she opened his stall door, he gave her a sour look.

"What? No happy whinny of greeting?" Melanie pretended to be shocked, though by now she knew what to expect. Tribulation—Trib for short—had been Christina's pony until she outgrew him. Since Melanie was smaller than her cousin, the two were a perfect match in size as well as personality. Trib was as ornery as Melanie.

"No time for brushing, but I do have this." She took a chunk of carrot from her back pocket. Instantly his ears pricked forward.

"I knew you loved me," Melanie teased, and giggled as he took the carrot. She put the reins over his head and, when he was through chewing, put the bit in his mouth.

"No racing ahead," Melanie told Kevin when she led Trib outside. "Trib might buck me off."

"Would I do something like that?" Kevin asked.

"Yes." Melanie put on her helmet. Gathering the reins, she tried to imitate Kevin's mount. Only when she jumped up, she plopped across Trib's back and hung there like a sack. She grasped his mane with her left hand, pushed on his rump with her right, then swung her right leg over. When she finally sat up, her cheeks were flushed.

Kevin had his head down, trying to hide his laughter.

"Make sure you buckle those helmets," Ashleigh said as she strode over. She took hold of Trib's reins. "There's a phone call for you, Melanie. It's your dad. You can take it in the barn office."

"Dad?" Melanie was puzzled, then delighted. They'd had such a good time this weekend, and she bet he was calling because he missed her.

Swinging her leg over Trib's rump, she dropped to the ground and ran into the office. The phone receiver was lying on the desk.

"Hey, Dad! What's up?" Melanie said when she picked it up.

"Hi, honey. Hey, I have terrific news," her dad replied.

"What?"

"Susan and I are getting married this weekend. We're going to be a family again. Melanie, it's time for you to come home to New York!"

JOANNA CAMPBELL was born and raised in Norwalk, Connecticut and grew up loving horses. She eventually owned a horse of her own and took lessons, specializing in open jumping. She still rides when possible and started her two young granddaughters on lessons. In addition to publishing many books for young readers, she is the author of four adult novels. She has also sung and played the piano professionally and owned an antique business. She now lives on the coast of Maine with her husband, Ian Bruce. She has two children, Kimberly and Kenneth, and three grandchildren.

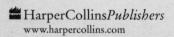

THOROUGHBRED

created by Joanna Campbell

Read all the books in the Thoroughbred series and experience the thrill of riding and racing, along with Ashleigh Griffen, Samantha McLean, Cindy McLean, and their beloved horses.